# PICTURE THAT!

**Bernice Wells Carlson**

Illustrator and Art Advisor
Dolores Marie Rowland

Abingdon
Nashville

# PICTURE THAT!

*Library of Congress Cataloging in Publication Data*

Carlson, Bernice Wells.
  Picture that!

  Bibliography: p.
  Includes index.
  SUMMARY: Folk tales and stories are introduced by related dramatic activities and followed by
art projects.
  1. Creative activities and seat work—Juvenile literature. 2. Handicraft—Juvenile literature. 3.
Tales. [1. Amusements. 2. Folklore. 3. Short stories. 4. Handicraft] I. Rowland, Dolores Marie. II.
Title.
LB1537.C37          372.5          76-25813

ISBN 0-687-31419-4

"How Napi Made the Animals" is from INDIAN TALES FOR LITTLE PEOPLE by W. S.
Philipps, © 1928 by Platt & Munk Company.

MANUFACTURED  BY  THE  PARTHENON  PRESS  AT
NASHVILLE,  TENNESSEE,  UNITED  STATES  OF  AMERICA

*Dedicated to*
*Bernice's youngest grandchild,*
*Cynthia Barrie Carlson,*
*and*
*to Dolores' parents,*
*Estelle and Vito Resta*

# Acknowledgments

First of all I should like to thank Dolores Marie Rowland, art teacher in the elementary schools of Bridgewater, N. J., who as my art advisor did much more than illustrate *Picture That!* She helped select art activities that capture the spirit of each story and are within the range of ability of children for whom this book is written, checked directions to make sure that almost any reader can follow them successfully, and compiled the bibliography of art books.

We should like to thank the many boys and girls who helped us prepare this book over a period of years—children in public schools, church-related programs, library storytelling groups, summer recreation activities, a residential camp, a preschool program, Brownie Scouts and Cub Scouts, and three Carlson grandchildren, Nancy, David, and Robert Umberger.

We should like to thank teachers and librarians who have offered advice and also people who helped us find, and in some cases translate, appropriate tales from other lands, especially Dr. Alexis J. Panshin, Okemos, Mich.; Yoshiko Yokochi Samuel, Yellow Springs, Ohio; Märta Villner, Mariefred, Sweden; José Carvalho, Vineland, N.J.; Carol Carlson, Yardville, N.J.; Sarah Gordon, Highland Park, N.J.; and Lois Howe, Franklin Township, N.J.; and Estella S. Resta and David H. Rowland, both of Franklin Township, N.J., who provided special help in gathering other types of background information.

# Contents

# Introduction

Some things just seem to go together: bacon and eggs, pancakes and syrup, ice cream and cake. In each case one food adds flavor to the other without becoming an integral part of it.

In somewhat the same way, related dramatic play, stories, and art activities can be combined to form a program that adds up to better understanding, advanced sensitivity, and more development in skills than could be gained from doing any one activity by itself.

Because of the variety, this combination can be more fun than doing unrelated activities or a lot of one activity. The combination may also help children sense relationships between their lives and storybook life and develop their ability to interpret life through art activities.

Children can participate in these activities long before they are able to take part in a dramatic production or draw or paint a character in a story. Taking part in choral readings or pantomimes, children learn to express themselves through speech and movement. Using different art materials in a variety of ways, they develop a feeling for the importance and beauty of lines, texture, shapes, and colors.

The stories and activities in this book were chosen for children from nursery-school age through the early grades. Not all young children can do or will want to do every project. But with guidance they can succeed with some activities. In general, the easiest activities and the simplest stories are placed in the first part of the book, and the more difficult activities and longer stories are placed near the end.

This is an open-end book. Following each story are two or more suggestions for art activities. Unless a child is working alone, a leader must decide which activity a group will do.

There are no patterns and no diagrams. Children must follow basic instructions, but then they are on their own. Children are encouraged to use their imagination as they work. They can complete projects by drawing or painting details or by adding appropriate odds and ends.

Basic methods are sometimes repeated by being incorporated into more complicated projects. For example: the troll collage near the beginning of the book is simpler than the collage with a pixilated girl that is presented later. The string rubbing of a net is simpler than the leaf rubbing employed later. The crayon-resist-watercolor snow scene is simpler than the pixie scene using the same basic method.

Some art activities may be interchanged. For example: the rabbit puppet in the wild-rabbit story can be used with the magic-stick story. The paper-bag puppet on a stick could become a troll puppet instead of a giant.

Familiarity with the book and use of the detailed index will help those who want to change activities for reasons of their own or who want to reinforce a story in the minds of the listeners by using several art projects, each of a different nature.

This book can be used in many types of programs, including: enriched storytelling activities at libraries; Head Start and other nursery schools and day-care centers; schools; church schools and church-related programs; Brownie and Cub Scouts and other clubs; residential and day camps. And at home! A parent, an older brother or sister, or a grandparent can share the programmed fun with one child, with several brothers and sisters, or with children and their playmates on an ordinary day or on a special party day. Some children may want to read a story and do art work on their own.

However you use this book, encourage children to—

feel like characters in the story;

follow directions and then use imagination; and

PICTURE THAT!

## Introducing Speech and Other Dramatic Activities

To introduce a speech or other dramatic activity, first get the children's attention and then hold it. Allow no distractions. Make sure that children are seated far enough apart to allow them to move their hands, and in some cases their feet and bodies, without hitting one another. Ask them to put all papers, purses, or other things under their chairs or some where out of sight and feel.

10

# INTRODUCTION

If they are seated at desks or at tables, make sure that the tops are clear.

One way to introduce speech-participation activities is to explain the word *cue*, a signal that tells an actor what to say or do: the raised hand is a *cue* to be quiet. To demonstrate this, ask everyone to clap with the leader, then stop the second he stops and raises his hand. From then on, the raised hand will be a cue to be quiet and listen.

If children are not familiar with pantomime games, the leader may choose to act out the first pantomime, asking the children to guess what is happening. If the pantomime requires two actors, the leader may ask an assistant to help out. Most children will soon offer to present their own pantomimes.

## Introducing Art Activities

Two rules for success in presenting art activities to children are:

1. Choose a story and related activities that you like and that you think the children will like because the story is within the range of their understanding and skills. The first story that you use should be related in some way to the children's experiences and knowledge gained from family, school and community life, television, or their own reading. Most children cannot picture something they have never seen or learned about.

As you work with the same group, you may want to extend the children's experiences before introducing new units. You may want to take them on a field trip to a tree farm, zoo, beach, or other place related to the story. Before you read about an imaginary creature you may want to talk about the troll, ogre, pixie, or whatever, and show pictures. You may want to show movies of life on the sea coast, under the sea, or in the north woods in winter if you think such scenes would help children visualize a story. To succeed, a leader must develop sensitivity to children's backgrounds, personalities, and abilities.

2. Be prepared! Read directions carefully and get the steps clearly in mind. Make a sample to reinforce your understanding of directions. In some cases you may want to show the sample to the group. In other cases you'll want them to experience surprise. For example: let them see for themselves how a design appears with a string rubbing, or let them discover that watercolors will not stick to wax crayoning.

# PICTURE THAT!

Only inexpensive, easy-to-get materials are required for projects described in this book. If you are interested in other products on the market, experiment before you make a substitution. For example: brushing watercolor over wax crayoning gives an unusual effect because the water paint does not stick to the wax. Some paints, however, will cover wax crayoning. Certain types of instant-stick glue are dangerous for children to use because fingers can get stuck together. Certain glues give off gas harmful to the nervous system. Use common sense in choosing materials.

Collect and store a variety of scrap material such as buttons, string, used gift wrapping, scraps of cloth and construction paper, a wallpaper sample book if you can get one. The more scraps you have on hand, the more choices children will have in creating. Do consider your storage space and likelihood of using material. Don't be a pack rat!

When nature products are needed, ask children to collect them and bring them to class. Encourage them to find cones, seeds, weeds, leaves, or whatever is needed. Don't start a project until you have enough material.

Consider the mess factor of a project. Often it is a good idea to protect the top of a desk or table with newspaper. If children are using paste, paint, or other materials that can be messy, determine in advance if they'll need smocks to protect clothing, where they can wash hands, and so on.

Have all equipment and materials on hand, but do not put them on the desk or table or within reach of the children until you are ready to use the equipment. At the start of the story activity period, have tables and desks clear. Let nothing distract children as they do speech activities and listen to stories.

Before you start art work, ask children to imagine the specific part of the story you have chosen to have them illustrate. Talk about it. You may ask: "What colors do you see in a sunset?" or, "What do you think an old troll looks like?" "Think about the feathers on an owl or on any other bird. Do feathers go every whichway? Or do they lie in a pattern?" A few minutes spent in this type of recalling and imagining helps children to picture lines, shapes, textures, and color.

Explain the art activity. If you wish, show a sample. Pass out materials,

12

# INTRODUCTION

asking helpers to aid you if necessary. Don't allow interest in the story to wander as you get ready for a new activity.

Encourage children to be creative within the scope of the project. At the same time, don't let them get frustrated. Help individuals if they really need help. Let them do all that they can do. Let them enjoy success.

Praise children who complete a project to their own satisfaction. Help them think it's fun to PICTURE THAT!

# I. What Kind of Stick?

The leader holds up a yardstick or other kind of stick and asks, "What kind of stick is this?"

When someone answers "Yardstick" or "Measuring stick," the leader continues, "Correct. But if I use my imagination, I can pretend that this stick is lots of other things. Guess what my stick is now?" The leader pantomimes using the stick in various ways.

For example as: a baseball bat
a broomstick
a paddle
a tightrope walker's bar
a cane
an umbrella handle

The pantomiming and guessing should not drag. Before interest wanes, the leader says, "You see, we can pretend that a stick is lots of things. Now listen to the story of 'The Magic Lifesaving Stick.' "

# The Magic Lifesaving Stick

Porcupine met Rabbit on a road in Russia.

"Where are you going?" asked Porcupine.

"Home," answered Rabbit. "A long way from here. Down the road, over a brook, across a swamp, through a forest, and up a steep hill almost as high as a mountain."

"That *is* a long way," said Porcupine. "We should walk together. Walking together makes the road seem half as long."

So down the road they started, paying no attention to the path, just talking and walking and walking and talking and talking—until, wham! They fell, flop!

Across the road lay a long stick, straight as a pole.

"Stupid stick," said Rabbit. He picked it up and tossed it into the bushes. "Stupid stick!"

"Not necessarily," said Porcupine, picking up the pole and looking at it carefully. "This may be a magic lifesaving stick."

"Bosh!" answered Rabbit.

Down the road they started again, talking and walking, walking and talking.

Porcupine used the pole as a cane and looked at the road now and then.

Soon they came to a narrow brook that ran between steep banks.

"How can we cross that?" asked Porcupine.

"Easy," said Rabbit. He took a running jump and landed squarely on the opposite bank.

"Now you jump!" called Rabbit. "Throw away your stick and jump."

"I can't," cried Porcupine. "With my short legs I can't jump like you."

"Then we must say good-bye," said Rabbit.

"Not necessarily," said Porcupine. "My magic lifesaving stick may help me. Let me think."

Porcupine looked at the stick. Then he held it like a vaulting pole, backed away from the shore, and took a short run. He stuck the bottom of the pole into the middle of the brook and vaulted to the opposite bank of the brook.

Rabbit was dumbfounded. "What a good jumper you are!" he exclaimed.

"Yes," agreed Porcupine, "with the help of my magic lifesaving stick."

On they went. At last they came to a swamp. Porcupine stood near the edge, poking turf with his stick, trying to find a solid spot before he took another step. But Rabbit, always impatient, took a long leap and landed first on floating weeds, and then plopped into the water.

"Help! Help!" yelled Rabbit. "I'm drowning!"

"Not necessarily!" called Porcupine. "Grab the end of my magic lifesaving stick."

Rabbit grabbed one end of the stick. Porcupine held the other end. Then Porcupine pulled and pulled with all his might. Rabbit kicked his legs. At last the two animals stood on a firm patch of turf.

"Thank you! Thank you!" gasped Rabbit. "You saved my life!"

"Yes," agreed Porcupine, "with the help of my magic lifesaving stick."

Porcupine and Rabbit crossed the swamp after Porcupine had tested each patch of turf before either animal stepped on it.

Down the road they went again, talking and walking, walking and talking and talking, until they came to the edge of a deep dark forest.

"My! My!" cried Rabbit as he looked into the forest. "Vines and briers have grown across the path. We can't go in there until winter freezes the vines and covers the path with snow. We'll have to wait a long, long time!"

"Not necessarily," answered Porcupine. "Maybe my magic lifesaving stick can help us. Let me think."

Porcupine grasped his stick with both hands. Then, using it like a long dull knife, he pushed vines and briers aside. "Follow me," he called.

Through the forest the animals went slowly, not talking, carefully finding the path and following it until, suddenly, right before them stood a wolf!

"Aha!" snarled the wolf. "Just in time for my dinner!"

Porcupine stood solid, his quills on end.

"Not you, my prickly one," snarled the wolf. "But you!" He slapped one paw on Rabbit's back.

Poor Rabbit turned as white as winter snow. He shook like autumn leaves.

"Let me think," mused the wolf. "Shall I eat you from tail to ears or from ears to tail?"

"Help!" whined Rabbit softly. "I'm lost."

"Not necessarily!" yelled Porcupine. He grasped his magic lifesaving stick firmly and wham! He whacked the wolf on the buttocks.

"Owwwwwww!" howled the wolf, more startled than hurt.

Wham! Porcupine struck again.

"Owwwwwww!" howled the wolf as he ran through the forest. For the first time in his life he had been whammed on the buttocks.

"Thank you! Thank you!" gasped Rabbit. "You saved my life!"

"Yes," agreed Porcupine, "with the help of my magic lifesaving stick."

At last they came to the edge of the forest. There they saw a steep hill almost as high as a mountain. Near the top stood a lone tree.

"There's my home," cried Rabbit. "In a burrow under that tree! Follow me!" he called. Off he darted, one leap and then another and another. But the hill was too steep for fast running. In no time at all, Rabbit was worn out. He had to lie down and rest while

Porcupine trudged slowly up the hill, holding fast to his magic lifesaving stick.

"I can't make it!" cried Rabbit when Porcupine was near. "So near to home, and I can't make it. I must give up!"

"Not necessarily," said Porcupine. "My magic lifesaving stick may help us again. Let me think."

Then he suggested, "Let me go first. You can follow. I'll hold onto one end of my magic lifesaving stick. You can hold onto the other end. Together we'll climb the steep hill."

On they went, walking and walking without talking, until at last they neared the top of the steep hill.

Out from the burrow ran lots and lots of little rabbits.

"Papa!" they called. "Papa! You're home."

"My dear one!" sighed Mrs. Rabbit. "You are home!"

"Yes," said Rabbit, "thanks to Porcupine and his magic lifesaving stick."

"A magic lifesaving stick?" asked Mrs. Rabbit.

"Yes, a magic lifesaving stick." And he told her of their adventures.

"Oh," sighed Mrs. Rabbit, "I do wish we had a magic lifesaving stick."

"Take this one," said Porcupine. He handed her the stick.

"We can't take your stick," said Rabbit. "How can you get along without a magic lifesaving stick?"

"I'll find another," said Porcupine. "One can always find a stick."

"But a magic stick?" asked one of the little rabbits.

"I'll tell you a secret," answered Porcupine. "The magic isn't in the stick. It's up here." He pointed to his head. "And down here." He pressed his heart.

"A quick mind and a kind heart can turn anything into magic."

Porcupine said good-bye and started down the opposite side of the steep hill. And as he walked and walked he thought and thought.

"Walking alone makes the road seem twice as long, with or without a magic lifesaving stick."

—A Russian tale retold

## Fingerprint Animals

**Materials:** ink pad, paper; and for drawing—pencil, ballpoint pen, or thin felt-tip pen.

The animals in the story can be pictured with thumb- and fingerprints and a few line drawings.

Press your thumb on an ink pad. Put your print on a sheet of paper. This is the body of the animal. To make a head, press a finger on the ink pad. Put your print where the animal's head should be.

Draw ears, nose, mouth, whiskers, or snout—whatever the animal should have.

## Cotton Bunny

**Materials:** white paper, pencil, paste, cotton, construction paper, felt-tip pens if desired.

Fluffy bunnies greeted Rabbit when he arrived home.

To make a fluffy cotton bunny, first draw a picture of a rabbit and cut it out.

Cover the figure with paste. Press small wads of cotton onto the paste. Add paper eyes, nose, mouth, and whiskers, or draw them with colored felt-tip pens.

# II. A Great Big Something

(Leader and children pantomime actions, keeping rhythm of verse as leader recites. All say the refrain "Who? Who? Who?" and the last line together.)

A great big Something
Knocking at your door!
Who? Who? Who?

(Pantomime knocking until end of the refrain.)

A great big Something
Stamping on your floor!
Who? Who? Who?

(Pantomime stamping in rhythm of verse until end of the refrain.)

A great big Something
Groping in the air!
Who? Who? Who?

(Pantomime reaching here and there in rhythm of verse until end of the refrain.)

A great big Something
Looking everywhere!
Who? Who? Who?

(Pantomime looking one way and another, moving body in rhythm of verse until end of the refrain.)

(Speak slowly and in spooky voice.)
A great big Something
Then grabs someone!
Who-oo-oo?
You!
Boo-oo! Boo-oo! Boo-oo!

(Point to someone as you yell!)
(Draw out scary "boos" in long breaths.)

23

# Who Lost the Golden Charm?

Once upon a time, a very little woman lived in a very little house on the shore of a great big sea. Every day this very little woman went out of her house, locked her door, and walked and walked on the beach. When she was tired of walking, she sat down on a piece of driftwood in the shade of a great big rock.

She loved to scoop up sand and let the teeny-tiny grains run through her fingers. She loved to take off her long stockings and her very little shoes and wiggle her toes in the sand.

One day, while she was resting and feeling the sand, her toes touched something hard.

"Doesn't feel like a buried shell," she said. "Maybe it's a treasure." She leaned over and picked it up.

Treasure it was! There in her hand lay a golden charm, unlike any charm she had seen before.

"It's beautiful!" she sighed as she admired the design. She looked more closely at it and thought, "Who would lose a golden charm? I'll try to find out. If I can't find the owner, the golden charm will be mine! Now, whom can I ask?"

A great big turtle sat in the shade of rotting timbers, sunning herself with her head stuck out.

The very little woman ran to the turtle and asked politely, "Mrs. Turtle, did you lose a golden charm?"

At the sound of the very little voice, the turtle pulled her head back inside her shell.

"Evidently the turtle didn't lose the golden charm," said the very little woman. "I'll try again to find the owner."

Next she noticed a very little sandpiper, tip-tiptoeing along the beach at the line where the waves touched the sand.

The very little woman ran to the shoreline calling, "Sandpiper! Sandpiper! Did you lose a golden charm?"

At the sound of the very little voice, the sandpiper spread its wings and flew away.

"Evidently the sandpiper didn't lose the golden charm," said the very little woman. "I'll try once more to find the owner."

At that moment a great big crab crossed her path, running sidewise.

"Crab, did you lose a golden charm?" called the very little woman. The crab kept running sidewise.

"I tried to find the owner," sang the very little woman with glee. "I can't find the owner. So now the golden charm is mine. I'll put it on a chain and wear it like a locket every day.''

The very little woman put on her stockings and her shoes, ran home, put the golden charm on a very little chain, and hung it around her neck like a locket.

She wore the golden charm all that day, all that evening, and even when she went to bed.

''I love my golden charm,'' said the very little woman as she lay her head on her pillow, pulled the covers up to her chin, and tried to go to sleep.

But sleep she could not. One thought kept her awake, asking again and again, ''Who lost the golden charm? Who lost the golden charm?''

Even when the sky grew very dark, the very little woman could not sleep. Then suddenly—

She thought—

She feared—

She *knew* that something was moving around her room.

The very little woman sat up in bed, opened her eyes and saw—

A great big Something was floating here and there around the room, searching, searching.

It floated over her dresser and stopped a moment.

It floated over her bookcase and stopped a moment.

It floated over her nightstand and stopped a moment.

Then it floated over the foot of her bed and spoke in a very little voice, "Who found my golden charm?"

The very little woman looked at the Something, put her hands on the golden charm, and didn't say a word.

The great big Something floated over the middle of the bed, spread out a little, and said in a louder voice, "Who found my golden charm?"

The very little woman looked at the Something, clutched the golden charm, and didn't say a word.

The great big Something hovered directly above the very little woman, spread out a little more, and said in a very loud voice, "Who found my golden charm?"

27

The very little woman took off the chain, held out the golden charm and whispered, "I did."

The great big Something swooped down over the very little woman, spread out its arms, and yelled,

"KEEP IT!"

And then it disappeared.

In the morning, the very little woman put on her golden charm. She wore it every day. It was her very own.

—New version of an old tale

### Floating Ghost

**Materials:** facial tissues, long piece of thread.

The great big Something floated around the room. It may have been a ghost. Picture a traditional ghost garbed in flimsy white, or a pink ghost, yellow ghost, or any other color floating ghost.

Wad a piece of facial tissue into a ball. Put the ball in the center of another piece of facial tissue.

Tie a long piece of thread around the second tissue at the base of the ball, leaving one long end for hanging.

Fluff out the edges of the tissue paper.

Suspend the floating ghost.

### Ghost Mobile

**Materials:** round plastic can lid (the larger the better), string, four tissue ghosts (above).

Make a mobile by suspending four floating tissue ghosts from a round plastic can lid.

Punch four holes at equal distances from one another on the edge of the lid.

Cut four equal lengths of string for suspending the mobile. Put an end of string through each hole and knot it. Then tie the loose ends of string together.

29

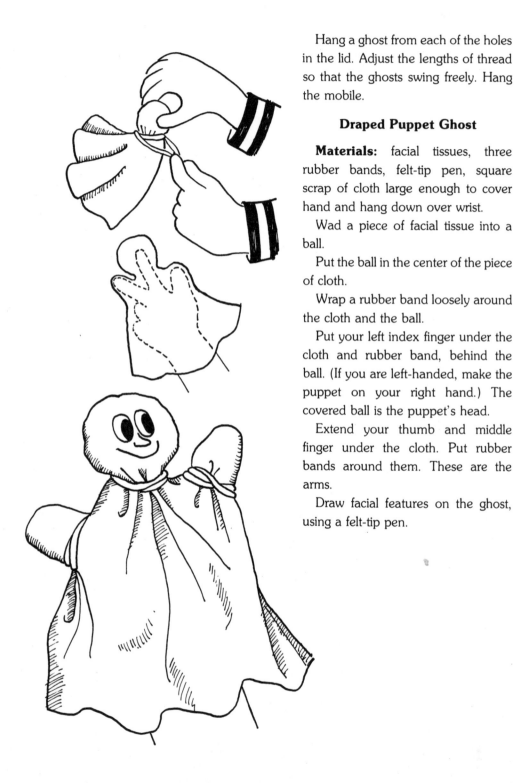

Hang a ghost from each of the holes in the lid. Adjust the lengths of thread so that the ghosts swing freely. Hang the mobile.

### Draped Puppet Ghost

**Materials:** facial tissues, three rubber bands, felt-tip pen, square scrap of cloth large enough to cover hand and hang down over wrist.

Wad a piece of facial tissue into a ball.

Put the ball in the center of the piece of cloth.

Wrap a rubber band loosely around the cloth and the ball.

Put your left index finger under the cloth and rubber band, behind the ball. (If you are left-handed, make the puppet on your right hand.) The covered ball is the puppet's head.

Extend your thumb and middle finger under the cloth. Put rubber bands around them. These are the arms.

Draw facial features on the ghost, using a felt-tip pen.

# III.  What's in the Net?

Before the game, the leader writes on filing cards or separate pieces of paper the names of three or four creatures that are easy to identify by their actions, for example: bird, elephant, horse, monkey.

When the group is together, the leader explains that they are going to play a pantomime game, a game where players act without speaking. The leader asks for a volunteer to pretend to be a creature that lives outdoors.

The leader shows the volunteer player the name on a card and asks her not to tell. If the player cannot read, the leader whispers in her ear. Experienced players may want to pantomime their own choices without suggestions.

The first time the game is played, the leader explains it as it progresses. The creature is asleep out of doors. The leader has a net and throws it over the creature. Then, for some reason, the leader lifts the net. (He may sneeze or turn at a loud noise or jump at the sight of a snake.)

The creature escapes and pantomimes running or flying. When the pantomime is finished, other players guess, one at a time, what the creature is. The better the pantomime, the easier to guess.

If no one can guess, other players may ask the actor questions that can be answered by yes or no such as: Do you live in a hot country? Do you eat meat? Do you climb trees?

Allow only three questions. Then ask the actor to give the answer and choose another player to be a creature. Play the game three or four times and then learn what Wild Rabbit, in the following story, found in his net.

31

# Why Wild Rabbit Stopped Hunting Game

Every morning, as soon as it was light, Wild Rabbit started to hunt. He always said, "First in the woods gets the game."

Some days he went to one place, some days to another. One day he went far to the east. There he saw tracks in the dewy grass.

"Mmmm," he said. "Who made those tracks?" He looked around but saw nothing. "Whoever you are," he shouted, "I don't like your tracks! I want to be first to hunt the game."

The next day Wild Rabbit rose very, very early. Again he went far to the east. Again he saw tracks in the dewy grass. No creature was in sight.

"Who is making those tracks?" he asked himself. "I have to find out."

Back he went to his burrow to talk to Grandmother.

"Something is hunting before I hunt," he told her.

"That could happen," said Grandmother, not very concerned.

"But I want to hunt first. I want to get the most game," said Wild Rabbit.

"I know. I know," said Grandmother. "But don't get excited."

"I'm going to make a trap," announced Wild Rabbit. "I'll catch that something!"

"Why?" asked Grandmother. "The something hasn't hurt you yet. You don't need the something. Why catch the something?"

"Because I have to catch the something that hunts first," answered Wild Rabbit, determined to do what he wanted to do.

Wild Rabbit went to the woods where he pulled down green vines. He twisted them this way and that way and tied them here and there until he had a big net. At one end of the net he tied a long vine rope. Then he pulled up tough, strong roots, soaked them in water until they were supple, and wove them into the net. Now the net was very big, very strong, and very cleverly made. Any creature that walked or rolled into the net would pull the opening together as it tried to escape.

Moving the net was quite a job, as Wild Rabbit soon discovered. However, he tugged and he pulled, and he pulled and he tugged. He dragged the net over rocks and through woods until at last he reached the spot where the tracks began.

Wild Rabbit laid the net in such a way that the

something making tracks just had to roll or walk into it. Then Wild Rabbit tied the loose end of the vine rope around a rock.

Wild Rabbit was tired after all the pulling, weaving, tugging, and dragging. No wonder. He had worked all day. It was getting dark. So Wild Rabbit went home, not saying a word to Grandmother about the trap that he had set for the something.

Very, very early the next morning Wild Rabbit rushed to the spot where the tracks began. Something was in the trap! Something big and round and hot. What could it be?

The sun! Wild Rabbit had trapped the sun. He ran home as fast as he could.

"Grandmother! Grandmother!" he yelled. "I caught the sun. What'll I do? I caught the sun!"

"Caught the sun?" cried Grandmother. "That's dreadful!"

"What'll I do?"

"Go back. Cut the net. Free the sun!"

"I can't! The sun's too hot!" wailed Wild Rabbit. "I can't!"

"You must!" said Grandmother sternly. "*You* captured him. *You* let him go!" Poor Wild Rabbit. He was so frightened that he just stood still.

Grandmother looked Wild Rabbit straight in the eye.

She handed him a hunting knife and said one word, "Go!"

Wild Rabbit took the knife and looked at Grandmother. Then he ran back to the sun as fast as he could.

"Untie me!" roared Sun. "Untie me!"

Wild Rabbit crept close to the ground. He reached out with his knife to cut the cord that held the sun. But the sun was so hot that Wild Rabbit couldn't breathe. He rushed back.

"Untie me!" roared Sun again.

Again Wild Rabbit tried to get near the sun. He

moved slowly and steadily, thinking that he might reach the rope gradually. But the sun was too hot.

"Untie me!" roared Sun. "I'll never touch earth again."

"All right!" said Wild Rabbit. "I don't care what happens to me. I'll do what I must do!"

Wild Rabbit grasped the knife firmly. He looked squarely at the vine rope to determine where to cut the line, took a deep breath, closed his eyes, and rushed to the spot where the rope held the sun. He quickly cut the rope and ran away from the sun.

Slowly, slowly, the sun rose in the sky where it has stayed ever since. It travels from east to west each day; but never touches the earth.

What about Wild Rabbit? He stopped hunting. He doesn't care who gets the game. Today he eats only green things and sometimes the bark on trees. On his fur, just back of his head, there's a yellow-brown mark. That's where Sun burned Wild Rabbit who caught him in a net.

—A North Woods Indian myth retold

### String-Rubbing Net

**Materials:** string, white paper, green and brown crayons with wrappers removed; and to hold worksheet steady—piece of cardboard and paper clips, and if you wish to mount the design—construction paper and paste.

Make a string-rubbing to picture Wild Rabbit's net of vines twisted this way and that, with little pieces of roots woven into it.

Set a piece of cardboard in front of you. Drop a string onto the cardboard, swirling it around to make interesting loops that cross one another here and there.

Lay a piece of white paper over the string. Secure this paper on the cardboard by placing a paper clip on each side.

Gently rub the white paper with the side of a green crayon. Dark green lines will appear as the crayon rubs over the string.

Remove the paper clips and lift the paper.

Move the string around a little to make a different design. Put the paper back in place on the cardboard.

Using the side of a brown crayon, lightly color over the string here and there.

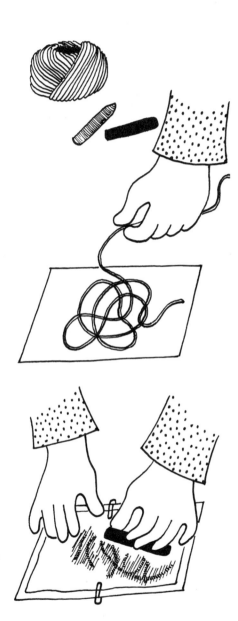

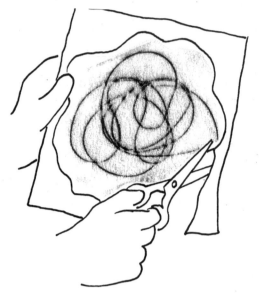

Remove the string from under the paper.

Using a dark green crayon, draw the uneven shape of a net around the edges of the string design. Cut it out. Mount the shape on a sheet of construction paper if you wish.

### Paper-Bag Rabbit Puppet

**Materials:** brown paper bag a little larger than a hand, pencil, crayons or felt-tip pens, brown construction paper or brown paper from another bag, staples; and for whiskers—strips of paper, pipestem cleaners, drinking straws, or wisps of dried grass.

Wild Rabbit can be pictured as a puppet that seems to open its mouth.

Flatten a small paper bag with the bottom folded down like a flap.

Put your hand inside the bag, placing your fingers inside the flap. Move the flap up and down with your fingers. Make a mental picture of a rabbit talking.

Lay the bag on the table with the flap up. Draw a rabbit's face on the closed bag so that the top of its head is on the top fold. Holding the flap down, draw a mouth so that the top half is on

the flap and the bottom half is on the main part of the bag just below the flap.

Color or paint eyes, nose, and mouth.

Cut long ears from extra brown paper and staple in place.

Make whiskers from strips of paper, pipestem cleaners, drinking straws, wisps of grass, or any other suitable material. Staple in place.

## Stitchery Sun

**Materials:** burlap, medium-weight cardboard, staples, chalk, heavy thread or yarn—and for sewing—a big-eyed needle, two matching buttons if your sun has eyes.

You can picture the sun with a stitchery design.

For a background, use burlap or any other loose-weave material. Cut this material the size you want your picture to be.

Staple wide strips of medium-weight cardboard around the edges to make a

39

stitching frame. This frame holds the cloth taut when you are sewing.

Using chalk, lightly draw a design of the sun on the burlap.

Thread a big-eyed, pointed needle with heavy thread or yarn. Tie a knot at the end.

Start any place on the design and push the threaded needle from the back to the front of the cloth. Outline the drawing by pushing the threaded needle back and forth through the cloth, from back to front, then from front to back, making a line of stitches that can vary in length. You will be making a running stitch.

# IV. The Troll

(Leader recites verse. Leader and children pantomime the action indicated.)

The Troll is walking,

   Thump, thump, thump! (Stamp feet three times.)

He sits himself on a

   Stump, stump, stump.   (Bounce up and down on seat three times.)

He says, "I'm hungry!"

   Glump, glump, glump! (Open mouth three times.)

"So I want something."

   Plump, plump, plump. (Pat stomach three times.)

He turns his body. (Turn body.)

Looks about. (Look.)

And then sees you! (Point to someone.)

Look out! Look out! (Duck down with arms over head.)

# The Troll and the Unearthly Noise

Long ago, in a rocky part of Sweden, there lived a farmer named Peter who owned a black cat named Murra and four goats.

One goat was red.

One goat was blue.

One goat was white.

And one goat was yellow.

Each of these goats had a special appetite.

The goat that was red ate pea soup and bread.

The goat that was blue ate applesauce goo.

The goat that was white ate potatoes fried right.

The goat that was yellow ate fruit, ripe and mellow.

The goats gave Peter lots of milk, and no wonder. He treated them well. He fed them all the special food they wanted, and every day he let them wander all over his farm and up on a hill nearby. But at night he locked them up, and for a good reason.

Under the hill next to Peter's farm there lived a mean, ugly, old troll who feared only one thing—an unearthly noise. He hated humans. And he dearly loved to gulp down animals that ventured onto his land

42

after sunset. Every night he devoured a quantity of wolves, foxes, mink, and, when he could find one, a bear cub.

But he didn't get Murra, Peter's cat; and he didn't get Peter's goats. They were locked inside the barn every night until, alas, one evening the red goat chewed and tugged on the latch string and somehow opened the barn door. The red goat walked out of the barn. The blue goat, the white goat, the yellow goat, and Murra followed.

At first they stood still and looked around. Although the sun had set, the sky was aglow with light.

"Beautiful!" said the red goat. He walked out of the barnyard. The others followed. He walked across the fields. The others followed. He walked to the hill where the old troll lived. The others followed. There, sure enough, stood the old troll.

"Who's walking on my hill?" shouted the old troll.

"I, the red goat," came the answer.

"I, the blue goat."

"I, the white goat."

"I, the yellow goat."

"Why are you walking on my hill?" demanded the old troll.

"Your hill?" asked the red goat. "This is Peter's hill."

43

"It's my hill!" cried the old troll. "I'll show you. I'll eat you up right now!"

"I'll kick you!" threatened the red goat.

"I'm not afraid of kicking," boasted the old troll.

"I'll butt you!" threatened the blue goat.

"I'm not afraid of butting."

"I'll bite you!" threatened the white goat.

"I'm not afraid of biting."

"I'll chew on your skin," added the yellow goat.

"I'm not afraid of chewing," boasted the old troll. "I'm afraid of nothing!"

"Nothing?" laughed Murra who knew a lot about trolls.

"Me-ow! Me-ow! Me-ow!" she howled. Murra knew that a troll is afraid of an unearthly noise.

On and on she howled. The troll grew pale. He turned green and grabbed his stomach. He'd lost his appetite for goats. In fact he threw up the mink, wolves, and foxes he had eaten.

"Me-ow! Me-ow! Me-ow!" howled Murra. All the cats in the area heard the howling, and they, too, began to howl. "Me-ow! Me-ow! Me-ow!" On and on they howled. Truly they made an unearthly noise. No wonder the old troll was frightened.

The troll covered his pointed ears with his hairy hands, but he couldn't shut out the noise. He turned and tried to run away from it, but wherever he went the unearthly noise continued.

"Me-ow! Me-ow! Me-ow!" Hundreds and hundreds of cats were howling.

The troll dashed through the woods as fast as his clumsy legs could carry him.

He stumbled on rocks.

He bumped into trees.

He ran to the edge of the mountain. He stumbled, lost his balance, fell over the cliff, and broke every bone in his body.

That was the end of the old troll.

Murra and the four goats went home where Peter
fed—

   pea soup and bread to the goat that was red;
   applesauce goo to the goat that was blue;
   potatoes fried right to the goat that was white;
   fruit ripe and mellow to the goat that was yellow;
and lots and lots of milk to Murra, the cat who led the
other cats in making an unearthly noise, a howling
weird enough to drive an old troll crazy.

(You can't blame the old troll for being afraid of an
unearthly noise. He was scared again and again when
he was a baby, hundreds and hundreds and hundreds
of years before. On every stormy night the great god
Thor threw his thunder hammer down from the sky
and hit trolls with a bang that shook the earth.)

                                       —A Swedish tale retold

## Troll Collage

**Materials:** construction paper for background, scraps of paper of various colors and textures, crayons or felt-tip pens, paste, glue if needed, and, if desired, such things as yarn or string, buttons, dry leaves, worn-out sandpaper.

Before you picture an ugly old troll by making a collage, imagine what he might have looked like. Maybe he had a big head and a little body. Or maybe he had a big body and a little head. Maybe he had two long arms for grabbing, or maybe he had three. Maybe he had long legs, or his feet may have been next to his body.

Maybe he had one eye or two eyes or three. The troll in this story had pointed ears. They may have been little or big and floppy. His nose may have been flat as a button, or it may have been long.

After you have formed a mental picture of the troll, cut out his head, body, legs, and arms from various kinds and colors of paper. (Or pieces can be selected from paper squares, ovals, rectangles, circles, and triangles that were cut earlier.) Arrange the shapes to form the troll figure. Paste the pieces onto background paper.

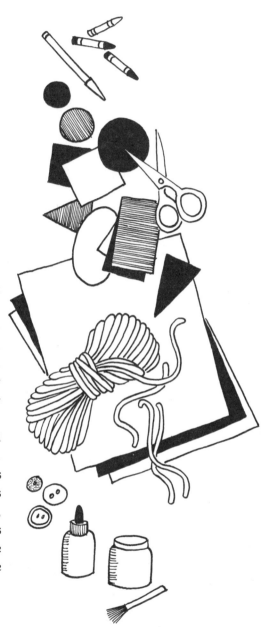

47

You can complete the troll in several ways:

Draw ugly eyes, nose, mouth, ears, and hair.

Cut features out of paper and paste them in place.

Use a combination of materials for features and hair. You can glue on buttons for eyes, paste or glue on yarn or string for hair, or paste on a long paper nose. To make the nose, cut a strip of paper and bend one end down like a tab. Paste the tab onto the face, and trim the strip to the desired length.

For a rough body, crumble dry leaves. Smear paste on the paper body. Press the crumbled leaves into the paste. Or cut worn-out sandpaper the shape of the body and glue in place.

Use your imagination to create an old-troll collage.

## Pinecone Troll

**Materials:** pinecone that is flat on stem end, heavy paper or felt, glue, other materials if desired, such as buttons, pipestem cleaners, bits of straw or dried grasses.

Stand a pinecone on its flat end. Look at it and mentally picture a shaggy creature. Think, "What can I add to this pinecone to make it look like a troll with a shaggy body?"

A pinecone troll needs not only a shaggy body but also feet, tongue, eyes, and hair.

Cut big feet out of heavy paper or felt. Put them under the cone.

Cut a long tongue out of red material. Tuck it into the cone, but don't glue it.

Make eyes out of paper, felt, buttons, twisted pipestem cleaners, or other material. Lay them on the cone, or at least plan where they should go.

To make hair, break pieces of straw or dried grasses into bits. Stick them into the top of the cone.

When the plan for the troll is complete, glue feet, eyes, tongue, and hair onto the cone.

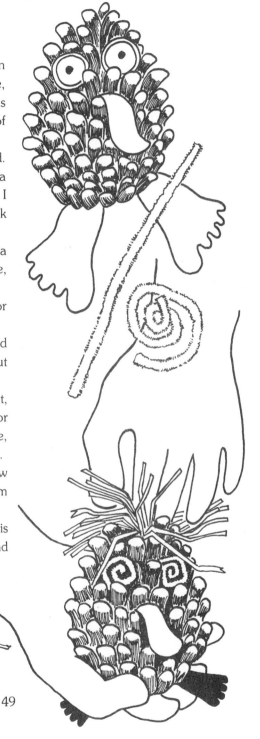

49

# V. Guess What I Want to Be

"Guess what I want to be," the leader might say in beginning this activity. "I'll pantomime something. Wait until I have finished acting and then guess what I want to be."

The leader then pantomimes either working or playing in a special way. For example, the leader may play a guitar. After the children have guessed what the pantomime is, she asks, "Who else would like to pretend to be someone different?" She chooses a volunteer.

"Wait," says the leader. "I'll wave my wand. The Wishing Breeze may help you become what you want to be." The leader pantomimes waving a wand and chants:

> Wishing Breeze,
> Diddle and Dee,
> Make Chad
> What he wants to be. (Of course, she uses the name of the child actor.)

The volunteer then pantomimes some action. When the pantomime is over, others guess what the actor wants to be. If children in the group have not had experience in this kind of pantomime game, the leader may suggest, by whispering in the volunteer's ear, some type of worker or player such as cowboy, ballet dancer, fisherman, piano player, carpenter, or baseball player.

Stop the game after three or four volunteers have done a pantomime, and read the story about a tree that made a wish.

# Glass Leaves on a Tree?

A spreading maple tree stood in the center of a small park. "Vest pocket" was a good name for the park, because it was indeed a small park, something like a little pocket in the crowded area where it stood. All around the park were old buildings. There were rows of brownstone houses, brick apartment buildings, and a wooden store building that had once been a stable for carriage horses.

Right across the street from the park stood a tall, modern office building made entirely of thick glass. Nearly everyone who passed that glass building stopped to look at it and talk about it.

"Look at that building!" they would say.

"Did you ever see anything like it?"

"How come they put it there? Sticks out like a sore thumb?"

"I rather like it," someone else might say. "It is spectacular."

"Agreed."

Whether they liked it or not, people talked about the glass building. Sometimes they would cross the street and stand in the park to get a better look at it.

"Here I stand, year after year," sighed the maple tree in the park. "No one talks about me. In the spring, I put out yellow-green leaves. In summer, my leaves turn dark green and give shade. In autumn, my leaves turn yellow, orange, and red, a pretty sight as they fall to the ground. In winter, my bare branches are silhouetted against the sky. Yet nobody talks about me."

Just then a couple sat down on the bench beneath the maple tree.

"At last," said the tree, "someone is going to talk about me." But no.

"Glad you spotted this bench," said the woman.

"Yes," said the man, "from here we get a good view of the building. Imagine a building made entirely of glass."

"Glass is spectacular," said the woman.

"Glass! Glass! Glass!" sighed the maple tree. "I wish my leaves would turn to glass. Then someone would notice me!"

The Wishing Breeze That Listens heard the wish of the maple tree, and, during the night, something unbelievable happened. The leaves of the maple tree turned to glass!

"What on earth?" cried a sanitation worker when he arrived at the park early in the morning. "What happened to that maple tree? It's leaves look like glass.'' He spotted a patrolman.

"Come over here!'' he yelled. "Look at that tree. Glass leaves!''

"Glass leaves? On a tree?'' questioned the patrolman. "Are you nuts?''

Then he, too, looked at the maple tree. "Now who would do a thing like that?'' he asked. "Turning a maple tree into a glass mobile. Some people like to tie knots, I guess.''

"These leaves aren't tied on,'' said the sanitation worker who was by now standing beneath the tree. "This tree is *growing* glass leaves.''

"Well, I never!" said the patrolman as he looked closely at the tree. He shook his head to make sure that sleep was out of his eyes. "I never did see a tree growing glass leaves. I'd better call my supervisor."

"And I'd better call mine. If anyone takes a potshot at those glass leaves, there'll be *some* sweeping up!"

"I'll call first," said the patrolman. "If there's hanky-panky going on, the chief should know."

He rushed to the first call box. "Officer Jones reporting. Corner 59th and 8th. Important. Let me talk to the chief."

"Impossible," said the officer at the desk. "File report in routine order."

"Right on. Get this. The leaves on the maple tree in Somers Park, between 58th and 59th streets turned to glass last night. Please investigate."

"Please repeat," said the officer.

"The leaves on the maple tree in Somers Park turned to glass last night. Please investigate."

"Right on," he answered. "Help coming at once!" He called the supervisor who in turn called the chief who in turn called the city's top psychiatrist who might be needed to handle a patrolman who thought he was looking at a tree with glass leaves.

Such a hurry and a scurry! The maple tree in the "vest pocket" park was the center of attention now!

People on their way to work. People out for strolls. People! People! People! All kinds of people gathered around the maple tree. Everyone talked about the maple tree with glass leaves!

Someone called the mayor. Someone called the botanical garden. Of course, someone called the newspapers and the television stations.

"Stay away from that tree! Don't touch that tree!" yelled police with bullhorns, as members of a crew roped off an area around the tree.

"Beautiful," cried some people.

"A hazard," said others.

"That tree will have to come out," ordered the commissioner of safety. "It's an attractive nuisance. Someone'll get hurt and sue."

"But a growing tree with glass leaves is a rarity. It should be moved to a protected spot," objected a horticulturist.

"You can't move a tree without permission from the Environmental Protection Committee," said the city attorney.

"Oh, dear! Why are they arguing?" sighed the maple tree. "I want people to say that I am pretty, glimmering in the sun like the glass building across the street."

"Let the tree stand until tomorrow. Post a guard all night," ordered the mayor.

The officials went away, but all day long people came to see the maple tree with glass leaves. The newspapers did "investigative reporting" and came to no firm conclusions. The television reporters interviewed spectators. For the first time in her life, the maple tree was the most talked of thing in the city.

Dusk came. The moon appeared. A slight breeze blew, and the glass leaves on the maple tree tinkled gently.

"Sorta nice," said one security guard to another.

"Real nice," agreed her partner. "Makes me sleepy."

Then suddenly everything changed. Big black clouds appeared. The entire sky grew dark, and a strong wind began to blow. People started running for shelter.

"Stay away from that tree!" yelled the guards. "Look out for that tree! It's glass!"

Crash! Crash! Crash! Glass leaves fell everywhere.

"Got to get more help!" yelled one guard. "Keep people away from that tree!"

"Operator!" yelled the guard at the phone. "Disaster area! Somers Park. Glass leaves all over the place."

"Repeat!" said the operator.

"Report. Disaster area. Somers Park," yelled the guard again. She slammed down the receiver and rushed back to help keep people away from flying glass.

"Dear! Dear! Dear!" wept the tree. "What have I done? I wanted to be a spectacular tree with glass leaves. Now I'm a disaster area. People will talk about a disaster area, but who cares? I wish, oh, how I wish! I want to be a regular maple tree again."

The Wishing Breeze That Listens heard the weeping tree above the tumult of the storm, and sometime during the night when all was calm, the maple tree burst forth with green leaves again.

"Where did all this glass come from?" asked a relief sanitation worker who had been sent to the Somers Park disaster area.

"Don't ask me," said his partner. "Glass building looks OK."

"Yes," whispered the maple tree to the Wishing Breeze That Listens.

"The glass building was built to stand the storm. I was meant to be a maple tree with leaves that fall gently to the ground."

"Do you have another wish?" asked the Wishing Breeze.

"Yes," said the maple tree. "I want to be the most beautiful maple tree possible. In the spring I'll put forth yellow-green leaves. In summer my leaves will turn dark green. In the autumn my leaves will turn yellow, orange, and red, and when they fall, they'll make a soft, pretty cushion on the ground, not trash like broken glass leaves."

People soon forgot about the tree with glass leaves. Day after day, city dwellers as well as tourists sat on the bench beneath the beautiful maple tree and talked about the spectacular building across the street. The maple tree was content.

—An old tale updated

## Leaf Rubbing

**Materials:** leaf, white paper, wax crayons with wrappers removed, construction paper and paste if tracing is to be mounted.

Choose a firm leaf. Look carefully at its shape. Feel the veins with your fingers.

Place the leaf on the table, veined side up, and cover it with paper.

Feel the veins and the edges through the paper. Now press the leaf and paper together with one hand.

Choose a crayon—a green one for spring or summer, an orange, yellow, or red one for fall. Using the side of the crayon, rub gently over the leaf. Gradually the shape of the leaf and its veins will appear.

To make a tree, shift the leaf under the paper. Rub with crayon again. If you are using fall colors, combine them. Keep moving the leaf and coloring it until you gradually see the general shape of a tree top. Draw a trunk and color it.

If the multiple rubbings of the leaf did not take the shape of a tree, outline a tree top on them. Cut it out. Paste it on another sheet of paper. Draw a trunk.

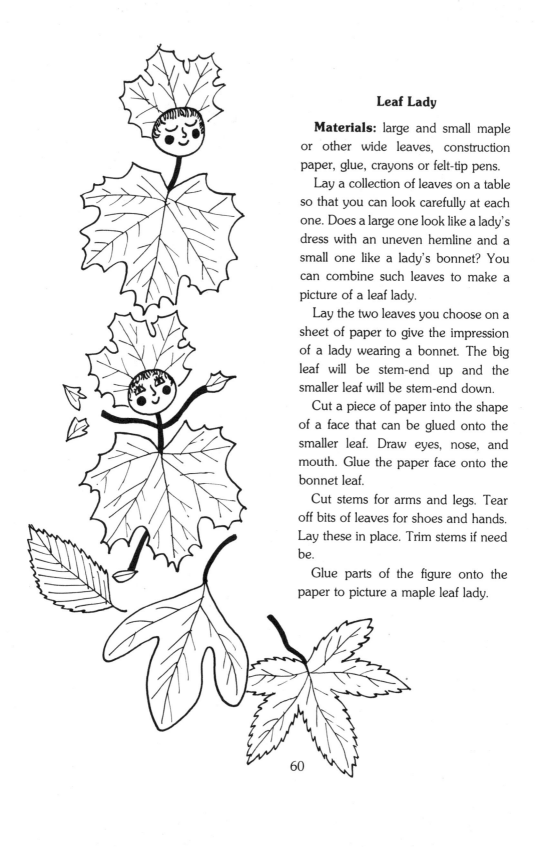

## Leaf Lady

**Materials:** large and small maple or other wide leaves, construction paper, glue, crayons or felt-tip pens.

Lay a collection of leaves on a table so that you can look carefully at each one. Does a large one look like a lady's dress with an uneven hemline and a small one like a lady's bonnet? You can combine such leaves to make a picture of a leaf lady.

Lay the two leaves you choose on a sheet of paper to give the impression of a lady wearing a bonnet. The big leaf will be stem-end up and the smaller leaf will be stem-end down.

Cut a piece of paper into the shape of a face that can be glued onto the smaller leaf. Draw eyes, nose, and mouth. Glue the paper face onto the bonnet leaf.

Cut stems for arms and legs. Tear off bits of leaves for shoes and hands. Lay these in place. Trim stems if need be.

Glue parts of the figure onto the paper to picture a maple leaf lady.

60

# VI. Sounds by the Sea

(The refrains of this poem rhyme. The gentle breeze in the pine trees says "Pish," with the *sh* sound drawn out. The waves are a little louder, with the *sh* sound still drawn out, "Swish." The sound of fairies is soft, "Wish." The leader reads the verse. Listeners join in the refrain.)

The breeze
In the trees
Says "Pish-sh, pish-sh, pish-sh."

The waves
In the caves
Say "Swish-sh, swish-sh, swish-sh."

The fairies
In the breeze,
In the trees,
On the waves,
In the caves
Say "Wish-sh, wish-sh, wish-sh."

# The Stolen Charm

Jiro sat on the sand at the foot of an old pine tree that grew on the shore of Sagami Bay.

"Pish, pish," whispered the pine tree as the spring breeze swept through its needles.

"Swish, swish," said the waves as they chased one another up to the yellow sand and threw white foam at the feet of the boy.

Jiro heard the whisper of the pine tree and the splash of the waves, but he looked far out over the water. He was looking for the white Foam Fairy who came each day to play with him.

At last she came, riding on top of the highest wave. In her hand she held something that shone in the sun like a drop of dew.

She sat down on the sand with Jiro. For a long time they sat watching the waves and the sea birds and the soft white clouds.

Finally she said, "Little boy, we have played here together for many weeks. Now I must go away to another land. I must say good-bye, but I want you to remember our happy times together."

Jiro nodded. How could he forget the happy times?

"Do you see this tiny silver ship?" the Foam Fairy continued. "I brought it for you. It is a charm and will always keep you well."

Jiro looked up to say good-bye, but all he could see was a rainbow that gleamed in a spray of the waves. The Foam Fairy was gone, but close by his hand lay a tiny silver ship that shone in the sun like a drop of dew. The boy picked it up and walked slowly to his home.

"See, Mother," he said, "here is a tiny silver ship that the Foam Fairy gave to me."

"That is a charm, my boy," said his mother. "You must keep it always, for it is most precious."

The boy showed the charm to his two pets, a furry Fox Cub and a fuzzy Puppy. They sniffed and blinked at it wisely, as though they knew all about it.

Weeks passed, and spring warmed into summer. One evening Jiro became very ill. His mother went to get the silver charm that would make him well. It was gone! Where could it be?

Furry Fox Cub and fuzzy Puppy sat in the dusk and blinked at the fireflies flashing among the trees. They thought of their sick master and wondered how they could help him.

At last Fox Cub said, "Ogre must have stolen the charm. Let's go and see."

"Oh, no! I'm afraid of ogres," said Puppy with his tail between his legs. "Besides, how can we get the charm if the Ogre has it?"

"Come along," said Fox Cub. "We'll find a way."

They crept softly along the path that led up the hill to the house of Ogre. On the way they met Rat.

"Where are you going?" squealed Rat.

"We are going to the house of Ogre to see if he has stolen our master's charm," said Fox Cub.

"I don't know how we'll get it if he has it," whined Puppy with his tail between his legs.

"I'll come along," offered Rat. "I know how we can get the charm if the Ogre has it. Wait here by this pine tree while I creep up to the house. When I am by the window, make a terrible noise. Then run for your lives! I'll meet you at the bottom of the hill.''

"I'm afraid," sniffed Puppy, his tail between his legs.

"Be brave!" said Fox Cub.

They waited by the pine tree until Rat had reached the window. Then they made noises, like all kinds of monsters, and turned and ran for their lives to the bottom of the hill.

Rat joined them shortly. "I know where it is!" she cried. "Ogre has the charm, and he keeps it in the pocket of his sleeve. I know it's there. When you screamed, he grabbed his sleeve and felt the pocket to make sure that the charm was still there. We'll wait until Ogre has calmed down and then go get the charm.''

"How?" asked Puppy.

"Follow me," answered Rat. When they were again by the pine tree, Rat said, "Now, Fox Cub and Puppy change yourselves into little girls. Then go into the house and dance for Ogre. Dance for your lives, and keep dancing until I am down the hill again.''

"I'm afraid of ogres," said Puppy.

"Be brave," said Fox Cub.

In a second Fox Cub and Puppy were little girls. Rat hid herself in the folds of Puppy's kimona. The two little girls walked to the door of the house, bowed when they met Ogre, and asked politely, "Please, Mr. Ogre, may we dance for you?"

Now Ogre was very tired and very cross, so a dance was just what he wanted to see.

They danced their very best and Ogre was so interested that he did not see Rat creep across the floor and up the sleeve of his kimona. He did not hear Rat gnaw through the cloth. He did not feel Rat grab the tiny silver ship. He did not notice Rat when she darted away with the charm in her mouth.

When Rat was safely out of the house, the dancing girls disappeared. Ogre never knew what became of them. When he looked out his door, all he saw was a fox cub and a puppy running and tumbling down the hill as fast as they could.

Fox Cub and Puppy met Rat at the bottom of the hill. They thanked her and ran to their master with the ship.

"Dear master," they called, "here is your charm. Now you will be well again."

Sure enough, Jiro did get well and lived long after furry Fox Cub had become a fox and fuzzy Puppy had become a grandfather dog with a strange habit. He put his tail between his legs whenever he heard *ogre*.

—Edited from *Japanese Fairy Tales* by
Teresa Pierce Williston

## String Painting of Flowers and Weeds

**Materials:** string, tempera paint, typewriter paper.

The flowers and weeds along the shore of a Japanese sea can be pictured by making a string painting.

Put some paint in small paper cups or small aluminum foil dishes.

Fold a piece of typewriter paper in half. Open it.

Dip a length of string into the container of paint, keeping one end clean.

Hold the string full length over either half of the paper. Now, lower the string so that it swirls on the paper like an *S*. Leave the clean end of the string off the paper.

Refold the paper. Place one hand firmly on top. With the other hand take hold of the loose end of string and pull it out, moving it around while still pressing the paper with the other hand.

Open the paper. The design should look something like a Japanese painting of weeds and flowers.

Dip another piece of string into a different color of paint. Lower it onto an unpainted area on the same side of the paper as before. Repeat the above process.

Add more designs if desired.

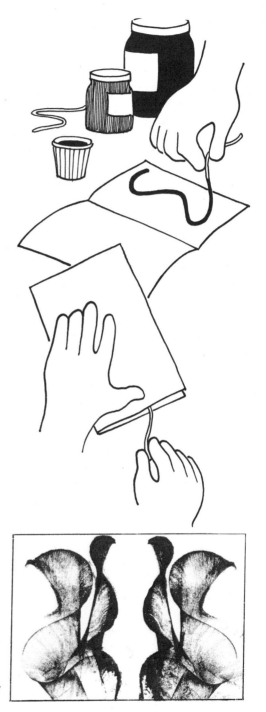

67

## Ogre Paper-Bag Mask

**Materials:** large paper bag, crayons or tempera paint, paper, staples; if ears are desired—drinking cups or paper plates; if hair is desired—yarn, string, or discarded fabric.

By tradition, an ogre was a wicked creature with a most distressing habit of changing himself into different shapes. In "The Stolen Charm" he chose to appear as a man.

To make a Japanese ogre mask, the artist first places a large paper bag over his head. Another person cuts away some of the bag at the sides to make it fit over the shoulders and then marks with crayon dots the position of eyes, nose, and mouth.

The artist can then take off the bag and begin creating the mask.

Cut out holes for eyes, nose, and mouth. Color around the holes, pressing the crayon firmly in order to get strong colors, or paint with tempera.

Think of additional ways to make the ogre look ugly. You might—

cut from paper a long tongue and staple it to the bag so that it hangs down on the chin;

make big ears from paper cups or paper-plate halves, staple in place;

make hair and mustache using yarn or string or strands of discarded fabric. Use your imagination!

68

## Rock Ogre

**Materials:** rocks, household glue, board for a base; if desired—paint or felt-tip pens, scraps of yarn, pipestem cleaners, drinking straws, dried grass or straw.

Collect rocks that are shaped like the body, head, and feet of a creature. Sometimes you can find a jagged rock that seems to have a nose, eyes (or one eye), and mouth carved by nature.

Wash and dry the rocks you plan to use. Pile them on top or next to one another to form a rock ogre.

Mount the rocks on a wooden base with household glue. First glue the bottom rock onto the board and then the others on top or next to it, according to your plan. Let the glue harden over night.

The ogre may be ugly enough with features carved by nature. Or you may want to draw features with paint or felt-tip pens. If desired, glue on horns and hair made of scraps of yarn, straw, pipestem cleaners, drinking straws, or other material.

(Note: Special glue, stronger than household glue, is needed to attach unsupported rock appendages, such as a nose.)

69

# VII. It's Christmas!

(The audience joins in the refrain saying "It's Christmas" in a slightly different way after each verse.)

Why bake lots of cookies and
    Fruitcake galore,
    Fill boxes for neighbors, and
    Then bake some more?
It's Christmas! (Softly and knowingly.)

Why deck out the house with
    Pine boughs and holly,
    Poinsettia, candles, a
    Santa Claus jolly?
It's Christmas! (A little louder and happily.)

Why festoon the tree with tinsel,
    Baubles, and lights that
    Sparkle and brighten
    Dull winter nights?
It's Christmas! (A little louder and joyfully.)

Why open the Bible and
    Read once again of
    Shepherds and angels,
    A babe, and wise men?
It's Christmas! (Softly and reverently.)

Why try to be joyful,
    More loving, forgiving;
    Make everyone feel that
    Life is worth living?
It's Christmas! (Loudly and with great spirit.)

# One Lone Juniper Tree

Many kinds of evergreen trees grew on the Jensen tree farm. There were blue spruce, white spruce, Norway spruce, Douglas fir, balsam fir, concolor fir, Scotch pine, white pine, red pine, and one lone juniper tree. Most of the spruce, fir, and pine trees were pruned each year to look like Christmas trees. A few that had grown crooked or had lost some branches were trimmed to give them pleasing, if not perfect, shapes. Only the juniper tree stood shaggy, with its prickly branches going every whichway.

"I ought to cut down that juniper," Mr. Jensen had said again and again. "I need room for seedlings."

"But you won't cut it down, will you, Daddy?" pleaded Jennifer time after time. "You know I love my juniper! I like one tree that's different."

"Besides," added her brother Steve one day. "Only the juniper tree has berries. The birds like the berries."

"Oh," laughed their father. "So the juniper tree is for the birds."

"So we'll keep it!" said Jennifer. "You promise, Daddy?"

"I promise," agreed her father.

In the fall, the Jensens put up a sign, Tag Now. Cut Later. So, day after day, during the crisp fall weather, people trooped up and down the rows of trees, looking at one tree and then another, each family trying to find the tree just right for them. As they walked, they talked about their Christmas plans and sometimes told the Jensens where the trees would be placed.

"That's the tree I want," one woman called out as she pointed to a spreading Scotch pine. "I want that tree for my living room."

"That's too big for a living room," advised Mrs. Jensen.

"Not for my living room," said the woman. "My living room is empty. That tree will be perfect in the center of the room!"

"I want a pine but not a Scotch pine," said one man.

"A red pine, like that one?" asked Mr. Jensen, pointing.

"Yes!" exclaimed the man. "That's it! Like the pine we had at home."

Few people noticed the juniper. One woman did ask, "Why do you keep a tree like that?"

"It's for the birds," explained Steve.

"Looks like it!" said the woman.

73

At night when the people had left and the moon shone bright, the trees began to talk to one another, as trees often do in legends.

"I am going to stand in the Van Ness homestead," said a beautifully shaped blue spruce.

"Aren't you rather high for a home?" asked a fir.

"For most homes, yes," answered the blue spruce. "But not for the Van Ness home. Ceilings there are nine feet high."

"I'm going to stand in a church sanctuary," sang a tall Norway spruce. "I thought I'd never be a Christmas tree. I'm too tall for a home. But what could be nicer than to stand in a church at Christmas?"

"To stand in a small apartment where there's a baby," answered a white spruce with one bare side. "I'm going to stand in a corner. My jagged side won't show. The baby will look at my lights and watch my plastic balls sway a little. I'll be the baby's first Christmas tree."

"I'll stand in a bay window," said a fir. "My family wants a perfect tree."

Even the unsold trees joined in the chatter. Each thought that one day he, too, would become a Christmas tree. Only the juniper was silent. He knew that no one would choose him for a Christmas tree. His branches were too shaggy. He was prickly to the touch. He didn't even smell like a Christmas tree.

Yes, he reasoned, he should be content. Jennifer and Steve liked him. The birds liked his berries. He knew that thousands and thousands of juniper trees stand in the woods and fields with no thought of ever becoming Christmas trees. But he, the one and only juniper tree on the Jensen tree farm, wanted to be a Christmas tree. But there was no chance! No way! The juniper was sad.

Christmas Eve was the saddest time of all for the juniper tree. Small flakes of snow began to fall. Birds sensed that a blizzard was on the way and settled early among the branches of the spruce and pine. As the night wore on, the snowflakes became larger and heavier. Soon they weighed down the tree branches. A wild wind blew, piling much of the snow into drifts. It snowed all night.

In the morning, everything was covered with snow. The birds that had slept in the pines and spruce began to fly about looking for food. It was hard to find. Seeds dropped from cones were covered with snow. Every berry that clung to a bush lay under a drift. Every seed-bearing weed was batted down. Only the berries on the branches of the juniper tree stood above the snow.

Birds darted in and out of the branches of the juniper, pecking at berries, leaving, returning. Then all at once, all the birds flew away together. They had heard the Jensens walking on the crusty snow.

"Look at the birds!" called Jennifer. "They're coming out of my juniper tree!"

"They were eating berries," said Steve.

"Having a feast," suggested their mother.

"That's right!" said Jennifer. "A Christmas feast on a Christmas tree. My juniper tree *is* a Christmas tree for the birds."

That night when the juniper tree could talk, he whispered to his neighbors, "At last, I, too, am a Christmas tree—a Christmas tree for the birds."

One bright star shown above the juniper, lighting up the very special Christmas tree—the Christmas tree for the birds.

—Bernice Wells Carlson

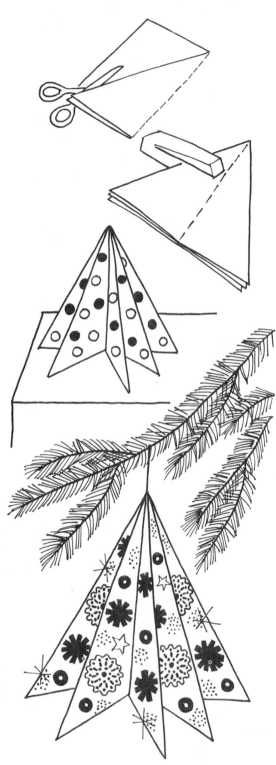

## Paper Christmas Tree

**Materials:** green construction paper, staples, glue or paste; for trimming—paper doilies, gummed paper, sequins or glitter; for drawing—pencil and ruler.

Fold a piece of green paper in half. Make a triangle by drawing a slanting line from the top corner on the fold to the opposite corner at the bottom of the paper. Cut along the line. Do *not* cut on the fold! The tree will be as tall as the fold is long and twice as wide as the base.

Cut out two more triangles just like the first. Open the folded triangles.

Lay the open triangles on top of one another with edges matching. If you are making a little tree, put the three trees together with one staple exactly in the center fold. If the tree is large, use two more staples.

Now hold the tree upright. Separate the triangles, so that each one extends from the center. Press where necessary to keep the space between each triangle.

Decorate the tree by pasting or gluing on pieces of paper doilies, gummed paper, sequins, glitter, or whatever you please.

The tree will stand alone on a table. Or you may add a string to it and hang it on a Christmas tree.

78

To make a fuller tree, use more than three triangles.

### Free-Flow String Ornaments

**Materials:** crochet cotton or thin string, household glue, wax paper, water, glitter if desired.

Free-flow string ornaments have a lacy look, something like snow and ice on a tree.

Place a small amount of glue in a container such as a plastic bottle top or a small aluminum foil pan. Dilute the glue slightly.

Cut a length of string and dip it into the diluted glue, being sure that it is covered.

Let the string fall on wax paper in swirls or other designs. Be sure that separate pieces of string overlap. Reinforce each spot where the strings cross with a drop of undiluted glue. Use as many strings as you need to create your design.

Sprinkle on glitter, if you wish, while the glue is still wet. Let the design dry over night. Remove it from the waxpaper. Tie on a string loop to hang the design on a Christmas tree. Small free-flow designs are especially pretty on miniature table trees.

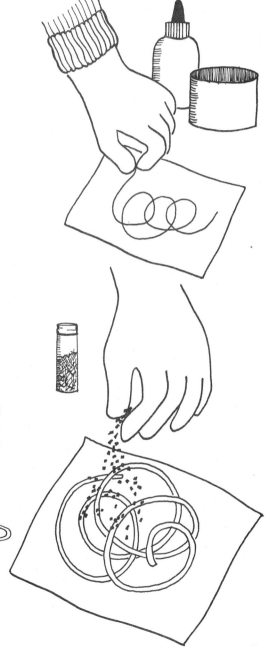

# VIII. The North Wind Blows

(Everyone makes the sound of the north wind after the leader
recites each line.)

The north wind is blowing.
Shoo-oo! Shoo-oo!
It blows on the bush.
Shoo-oo! Shoo-oo!
It blows on the tree.
Shoo-oo! Shoo-oo!
It blows on the house.
Shoo-oo! Shoo-oo!
And it blows on me! (Grasp arms across chest as if trying to
    keep warm.)
Shoo-oo! Shoo-oo! Shoo-oo! Shoo-oo!

# Shingebiss
# and the North Wind

Shingebiss, the wild diver duck, lived alone in a small lodge beside a bay of a large lake in the north country. Winter didn't bother him. He was prepared. He knew how to live with cold weather, and he liked it.

"I'm lucky," Shingebiss often said to himself. "I can keep warm and well fed in the worst of weather. I need help from no one."

For fuel, Shingebiss had four large logs, one for each month of winter. For food, he had fish that swam near the bottom of the lake. Shingebiss knew how to catch fish in winter.

Even on the coldest day, Shingebiss crossed the crusty snow that edged the bay until he reached a spot where rushes pushed through the ice. With his strong bill, he pulled up some of the rushes. Then, where the ice was cracked, he made a hole and dove down, down into the cold, clear water where fish were swimming. In a flash he grabbed a fish, surfaced above the ice, and waddled back to his home.

Once inside the lodge, Shingebiss blew on the fire to make it flare up enough for cooking fish. Content after his meal, he lay down and sang himself to sleep.

81

One winter the weather grew colder than ever before. The North Wind blew down with fury. He swept over the lake, freezing the water into deep ice. He brought blizzards of snow that he piled into great drifts. He watched with glee as deer and rabbits ran for shelter, squirrels holed up in hollow trees, and bears retreated into caves to sleep all winter. Only one creature remained in sight. Shingebiss, the wild diver duck, walked alone, dragging fish back to his lodge.

The sight of one creature unafraid of cold blistering weather made the North Wind furious. He watched smoke curl up from the home of Shingebiss and then began to howl.

> Shoo-oo! Shoo-oo!
> Shingebiss, I want
> You-oo-oo-oo!

Inside the lodge, Shingebiss sang a song of his own.

> Blow, North Wind, blow!
> I want you to know
> We were meant to live together.

Hearing the song, the North Wind pushed open the door of the lodge, entered the room, and sat in a far corner, blowing icy air all around the little duck. Shingebiss paid no attention to his unwelcome guest. He waddled to the fire, stirred the embers, sat down, and sang a second verse of his song:

Freeze, North Wind, freeze!
Freeze all you please.
We were meant to live together.

The North Wind grew more and more angry. He sat in his corner and breathed more cold air into the lodge. He panted and panted, and the more he panted, the brighter the fire glowed and the warmer the lodge became.

At last the North Wind could stand no longer the heat of the room and the duck's contented singing. So, he sulked out of the lodge and lay quietly waiting for Shingebiss to come outdoors and search for food.

In due time, Shingebiss left his lodge and waddled to his favorite fishing spot. It was covered with snow. He went to a second spot. Here, too, the drifts were high. So he went to a third place. Here, logs and other debris had formed a protective fort around a group of rushes. Inside the shelter, the ice was clear. Shingebiss pulled up rushes, chipped away the ice around the little holes, and fished to his heart's content.

The North Wind watched and waited for the best time to teach a lesson to the little duck who defied his might. "Perhaps," he thought, "If I lie quietly, Shingebiss will forget about the wind and grow careless. Then I'll catch him!"

At last Shingebiss started back to his lodge. He followed the sheltered edge of the bay as far as he could. Then he crossed a short stretch of open ice.

Suddenly the North Wind swooped down and blew directly on the back of the little duck who waddled on. A coat of feathers and down kept him warm.

The North Wind piled snow on the back of the little duck. Oil on the coat of feathers made the snow fall off.

Shingebiss waddled home and entered his lodge as the North Wind kept calling:

> Shoo-oo! Shoo-oo!
> Shingebiss, I want
> You-oo-oo-oo-oo!

The North Wind tried to blow the lodge down, but the lodge was too well built.

The North Wind tried to blow out the fire, but the fire kept burning brightly.

The North Wind tried to frighten the little duck, but Shingebiss kept singing:

> Blow, North Wind, blow!
> I want you to know
> We were meant to live together.

At last the North Wind gave up. Nothing could discourage the self-reliant Shingebiss.

Today the North Wind and the wild diver duck live together in the north country. The North Wind still howls:

PICTURE THAT!

Shoo-oo! Shoo-oo!
Shingebiss, I want
You-oo-oo-oo-oo!

The diver duck calls back,

We were meant to live together.
—An Ojibwa tale retold

## Snow Scene with Crayon Resist

**Materials:** white wax crayons, white paper, watercolor paint. Picture the snow-covered woods as they might appear on a winter night in the north country.

Using a heavy wax crayon, draw trees with bare branches or evergreen trees white with snow, grasses, shrubs, snowdrifts—whatever you want in the picture. Press hard on the crayon so that wax will stick on the paper.

If you work on a rough surface, such as a board or an old table, the trees and ground in the drawing will appear to have a rough texture.

When the picture is complete, paint over it with black watercolor. Use wide strokes going in one direction. Do not paint back and forth and around and around or up and down making an overly wet mess. Because the watercolor will not stick to the wax, the white wax drawing becomes silhouetted against a dark background.

To make a snowy-day scene, add white clouds or snowflakes to a white crayon drawing. Paint the upper half of the picture blue for the sky and the bottom portion brown for the earth and rocks made bare as the wind blew snow into drifts.

## Diorama

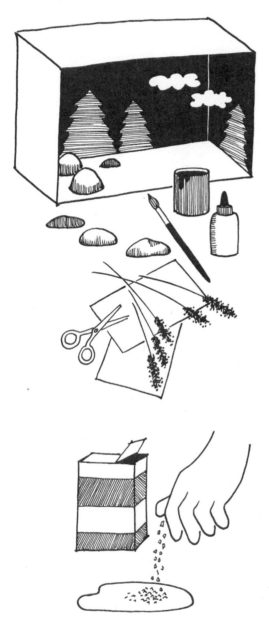

**Materials:** shoe box, paint, paper, salt (kosher if possible), paper clips, paste, glue, other materials such as pebbles, greens, twigs, dried grasses, modeling clay.

A *diorama* is a scene with a painted background with figures standing in the foreground. This woodland scene with a lake, woods, and a little duck may be made entirely of paper, paint, and paste, or it may contain a combination of materials including pebbles, twigs, dried weeds, moss, a duck modeled of clay.

There is no need to complete a diorama in a day. You can make the background scene and then add other materials when you find just the right things such as pebbles that will look like miniature rocks.

To start a diorama, lay a shoe box on one side with the opening facing you. Paint a background picture of sky and trees inside on the back and sides.

Cut out a piece of white paper the size and shape of the lake needed in the scene. Cover it with paste and sprinkle salt on it. Kosher salt and some kinds of pickling salt are best because they have coarse crystals that look a little like ice.

Draw and cut out a little duck with a tab on the bottom. Bend the tab back. If you put a paper clip on the tab, the figure will stand up. Make construction-paper trees, each standing on a tab like the duck.

Now, plan your winter scene. You can move the duck and trees about as you do this.

Remove the clips when you are ready to paste the figures in place.

For a more elaborate scene, gather fresh greens, twigs, dried grasses, and other natural materials. After trimming them to the sizes and shapes needed, stick them into little balls of modeling clay so they will stand up. Collect pebbles that look like miniature rocks. The little duck can be modeled of clay.

When everything is ready for the scene, paste the lake in place. Paste and glue figures in place. Stones can be attached to the box and to one another with household glue.

89

# IX. What Can You Do?

(Children follow the motions of the leader.)

If pixies come, you'd better watch out;
For strange things happen when they're about.
They rap on walls. Bang, bang, bang! (Rap three times.)
The pots fall down. Clang, clang, clang! (Make falling motions.)
The bread and ham move around the table. (Make circular motions.)
The riding horse runs out of the stable. (Motion swiftly to side.)
A chair will chase you around the room. (Make circular motion.)
You'll use a dish mop like a broom. (Make low sweeping motion.)
You'll be PIXILATED!
What can you do?
Listen to the story and find out.
(After the story, repeat the verse, and have children answer the question: What can you do?
Turn your pockets inside out.)

# *Pixilated!*

It was a mystic hour in Cornwall, that special time of day at a certain time of year, when the sunset lingers and turns the sky to rainbow colors. Blues, pinks, yellows, greens, flowed together with no dark grays in sight. A shaft of light cut through the sky and shone like a spotlight on the rocks and meadows that lined the dusty road. Down in the grass, crickets chirped; and in the pond frogs croaked like an orchestra in front of a lighted stage. It was a time when something strange was sure to happen. But Sylvia didn't think about that.

Sylvia sang as she walked down the road that led home. Her heart was happy and her feet were light. All her thoughts were about her wonderful day at the fair. She had sold her wares early—and at a good price. With her new money she had bought a pot, a beautiful pot, a proper pot for her hope chest.

"Hope to marry whom?" she mused. "Who knows? A Jack no doubt; for Jack is a proper Cornish name. There are lots of Jacks in Cornwall. Certainly one Jack will marry me. That's why I need this pot. In this pot, I'll mix his pasty dough. And in this pot—"

For no known reason, she dropped the pot. It landed with a clank on the road.

"My poor pot," moaned Sylvia as she picked it up. "Maybe my right arm is too tired to carry you. I'll carry you in my left."

So she put the pot in her left arm and started down the road again, between the rocks and meadows still bright with the setting sun. But before she had a chance to look to the left or right, she dropped the pot again.

"Clumsy me!" she said. "My arms must be very tired. How can I carry my new pot? I know. I'll put it on my head."

Sylvia stood very straight and placed the pot squarely on her head. She kept her eyes straight ahead, not looking left or right, and walked slowly down the road. But in spite of her caution, the pot slipped and started to fall. She caught it just in time.

"Thank goodness!" sighed Sylvia. "No more bumps on my precious pot. I guess I'll have to tie it around my neck with my apron strings and carry it home on my back. I'll look like a peddler, but who cares at a time like this? My day was lucky. The world is beautiful. The sky is bright. Crickets and frogs are singing. The meadows—"

Sylvia looked around. There were no meadows. She was on a strange road. On her left was a pile of stones, the ruins of an ancient building. On her right were rocks. She looked down the road ahead. No familiar landmarks lined the way.

"Where am I?" she called in fright. "I'm on the wrong road! How did I get on the wrong road? I must turn around and go back to a crossroad."

Sylvia turned, but she couldn't move. Her feet felt tied. Well, not tied exactly. Something was in her way. All she could do was kneel. So kneel she did; and down there on the road she saw the strangest sight.

All around her were tiny people, the smallest and the most unusual people she had ever seen. The little men wore red breeches, like gentlemen of long ago, grass-green frock coats, and stocking caps with tassels that hung down their backs. The little women wore long dresses with grass-green skirts and red bodices, big white aprons, and muslin caps—all very proper.

"Please! Please! Get out of my way," begged Sylvia. "Look! The sun is setting. I must turn around and go home quickly. I don't want to walk home in the dark."

The little people laughed and danced around and around Sylvia to the tune of crickets and frogs.

"Please," begged Sylvia. "I'm on the wrong road. I must get home. I don't know how I got on the wrong road."

The little people nodded their heads as if to say "We

93

know'' and laughed and danced around and around Sylvia to the tune of crickets and frogs.

Sylvia tried to step over the little people; but she could not. She tried to dodge the little people; but she could not. She tried to stampede through the little people; but she could not. Somehow they managed to dance around and around her in a way that stopped her from going on.

"Please! Please!" she begged. "I have a new pot. I must get it home safely. I don't know why, but again and again I dropped my pot on the road."

The little people nodded as if to say "We know" and danced on and on around Sylvia.

"If you won't let me go, will you tell me who you are?" begged Sylvia. The little people shook their heads and danced on and on.

"I feel pixilated!" screamed Sylvia.

For just a moment, the little people stopped, stared at Sylvia, stared at one another, and then danced on, around and around Sylvia.

"I know!" cried Sylvia. "You are pixies. You led me onto the wrong road." The little people nodded and continued to dance.

"You made me drop my pot." The little people nodded.

"You want some bread." The little people nodded.

"I have no bread. You want water." The little people nodded.

"I have no water. What can I do?" The little people danced on and on to the tune of crickets and frogs.

Once again Sylvia tried to step over them, dodge them, stampede through them. But the little people would not let her go. Sylvia could do only one thing—stand still and think.

"What did Grandma tell me about pixies?" she asked herself.

"'They dance to the tune of crickets and frogs.

They'll lead you onto the wrong road.

They'll make you drop your pots and pans.

They like bread. They like water.
They'll play tricks on you.
The only way to make the pixies go away is—'
Now I remember," cried Sylvia. "Grandma said,
'If you meet a band of pixies,
　And they bother you,
Turn your pockets inside out.
　Then they will skiddoo.'"

So Sylvia did just that. She turned her pockets inside out. The pixies disappeared. Sylvia ran back down the road and turned the right way at the crossroad. She reached home just as the last shades of pink, yellow, and blue left the sky and the stars and moon came out. She was pixilated no longer.

—Based on Cornish folklore

## Sunset Scene with Crayon Resist

**Materials:** watercolor paints, wax crayons, white paper; if collage is desired—construction paper, paste.

Picture an evening when the sky is filled with color. Imagine that pixies are dancing. Use the crayon-resist-paint method to depict the scene.

Toward the bottom of a piece of white paper, color with wax crayons tiny pixies in a semicircle. At the sides of the picture, color firmly with the crayons some dark rocks and ruins of a stone building. Do not color what is to be the road or sky.

Using watercolors and a very wet brush, paint at the top of the page bands of colors like the sky in the story. Keep the strokes going in one direction. Do not paint back and forth or around and around or up and down. Let the strips of wet color flow together.

When you reach the part of the picture where the pixies are dancing, change to brown color for the road and ground. Continue to paint across the picture in one direction, covering pixies as well as rocks and ruins.

Let the paint dry.

If you wish, you may add a collage. Cut from construction paper the figure of a girl. Cut out a pot.

When the paint is dry, paste the figures in place.

97

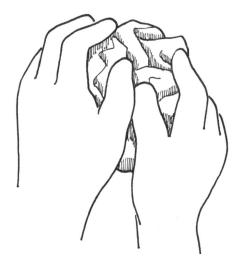

## Sunset Scene on Crumpled Paper

**Materials:** watercolor paints, white typing paper, construction paper of several colors, paste; for working—newspapers, sponge, water.

Sometimes a mystic sky seems to have blotches of pastel colors running together. You can achieve this effect by using the crumpled-paper method of painting. Then you can illustrate the story by making a collage against this type of mystic sky and mounting the scene on construction paper.

Before you start, cover your work space with newspapers.

Now trim the edges of a sheet of white typing paper so that it will be somewhat smaller than the sheet of construction paper on which you will eventually mount the scene.

Wipe the sheet of white paper with a wet sponge so that the surface is soaking wet.

Using a wide brush, dab light watercolors here and there on the wet paper. Use red, blue, yellow, green.

Crumple the painted paper into a wad. The colors will run together, forming new colors in interesting designs. Open the paper. Let it dry.

While the painted paper is drying, plan a collage scene. Cut out shapes of rocks and ruins, using different shades of brown, black, and gray construction paper. Cut out a brown road.

Lay the shapes in front of you to get a general idea of the picture you are creating. If you wish, add trees, shrubs, a girl, her pot, and other details.

When the crumpled paper is dry, arrange the pieces of the collage on the painted paper to make a scene with a mystic-sky background. Overlapping the pieces may give the effect you want. If you find you have made a figure too large or too small or a shape you don't like, discard it and cut another.

When your picture is complete, paste the pieces in place on the painted paper. Paste the scene on a sheet of construction paper which will provide a frame of color around the picture.

Note: In some situations, the leader may wish to talk about a mystic sky and have the children paint one at the start of the period. After the speech activity and story, the children can create their collages laying the shapes on the painted paper as they are cut out.

# X. When Napi Made the Animals

The leader says, "When Napi made the animals he made the—" A child names an animal. The leader then makes up a silly rhyme. The dialogue might run like this:

Some Indians who lived long ago in the Southwest believed that Napi made the animals out of clay.
When Napi made the animals he made the—(Child) cat.
A cat! Think of that. He made a cat.

When Napi made the animals he made the—(Child) horse.
A horse! Of course, he made a horse.

When Napi made the animals he made the—(Child) hippopotamus.
A hippopotamus! Glad it didn't sit upon us.

When Napi made the animals he made the—(Child) deer.
A deer! Never fear a deer.

Some rhymes may be forced. Don't worry. This is passing fun with a purpose. For example: A tiger! Don't try to ride her.
A monkey! He doesn't have a trunk key.

Note: If a leader feels unsure of his ability to rhyme on the spot, he may want to think ahead of time about how he would make rhymes for animals most likely to be mentioned. For example:

A dog—brown as a log.

A sheep—it couldn't say "Peep."

A lion—it went away cryin'!

A pig—it was big that pig!

If a leader is really stumped or wants to pretend that he is, he can ask the children for help. Some children make excellent rhymes quickly and should be encouraged to do so.

In some cases a leader may have to say, "I give up on that one!" and join in the laughter that is sure to follow.

# How Napi Made the Animals

Napi was large, oh, very large! He was the principal servant of the Sun in olden times when the Sun was a great fiery chief who lived in his lodge in the sky.

The Sun was busy all day long warming the earth, so Napi had to work fast in order to finish all the other jobs that had to be done.

One day, however, he finished his work early, and sat down by a spring to rest and smoke his long Indian pipe. While he sat there, he noticed some damp clay by the side of the spring. He picked up some of it and began to make queer shapes out of it. He made a great many of these shapes and put them all on a flat stone to dry. Then he sat and smoked and looked at them for a long time.

By and by he picked one up and blew his breath on it and said, "Go now, my son, and be a bighorn sheep and live on the plains."

Then he blew on the other clay shapes in turn and told them to be an antelope, a badger, a bear, a beaver, and so on, until he had named all the animals and told each one where to live.

Napi had one little clay shape left, and he looked at this one for a long time while he sat and smoked. After a while he blew on this one, too, and said, "Go now, my son, and be a man and live with the wolves." So, it is said, that is how the first man and first animals came to be on earth.

When Napi had made all the animals and had given each one a certain part of the country to live in, he thought he had done everything right and that all would be satisfied.

A few days later, Napi went to the spring again to rest himself. While he sat there smoking his pipe, all the animals came to him to complain. Buffalo spoke first, "Ho, Grandfather! You did not do things right after all! We are not satisfied."

"Why are you unhappy?" asked Napi. "I gave good land to each of you. Why do you complain?"

"Because," said Buffalo, "you told me to go up into the mountains. I cannot live there. There is no grass for me to eat. The hills are so steep I cannot climb them. The rocks break my hooves. That is not right, Grandfather. I cannot live in such a place."

Bighorn Sheep said, "Grandfather, I cannot live down on the plains. My hooves grow so fast they curl up. There is no moss to eat, so I am hungry all the time. There are no hills to climb, so my legs get weak."

Antelope said, "Grandfather, you told me to live in the mountains. I cannot live there, for the big rocks break my thin legs, and I cannot run fast because the hills are so steep."

Napi listened to the complaints of all the animals.

When he had thought everything over carefully he said, "Now, my sons, I will change you about, and give to each of you a country that will suit you. You, Buffalo, go and live on the grass plains and let Antelope live with you. You, Bighorn Sheep, go and live among the high mountains and take Mountain Goat to live with you. You, Bear, go and live among the timbered hills and let Cougar live with you. You, Wolf, live on the plains and let Badger and Prairie Dog live with you. Share your country and your meat with Man." So Napi told each animal where to live, and they have lived there ever since and been satisfied—all except Man. Man is never satisfied with what he has or where he lives.

—A Southwest Indian tale

## Clay Animals

**Materials:** modeling clay.

Napi's world was filled with sky, sand, plains, mountains, animals, and men. Some tribes of the Southwest pictured this world by modeling clay, painting on pottery, weaving, and making sand drawings. You may choose to depict a part of Napi's world by modeling animals of clay.

Work the clay with your hands to soften it. Get the feel of the clay and think, "What animal do I want to make?"

You may choose to use one of the following methods for modeling.

1. Shape the entire figure from one lump of clay by rolling, squeezing, and pinching it and pulling off excess pieces of clay until the figure has the desired shape of head, body, legs, ears, and tail, if the animal has one.

2. Divide the lump of clay into smaller pieces. Form the various parts of the body from separate pieces of clay. Then put them together, joining the pieces by blending the clay.

### Sandpaper Drawing

**Materials:** scrap paper, pencil, chalk, old wax crayons, sandpaper.

Coloring on sandpaper gives an effect similar to Indian sand painting. Make a sketch on scrap paper. You might draw a rabbit hopping in the desert or sheep grazing on the plains or maybe an Indian design.

When you are satisfied with the drawing, copy it with chalk on sandpaper.

Color the picture or design using old broken crayons. Fat crayons are best because, when scraped on sandpaper, they do not wear down as fast as smaller ones.

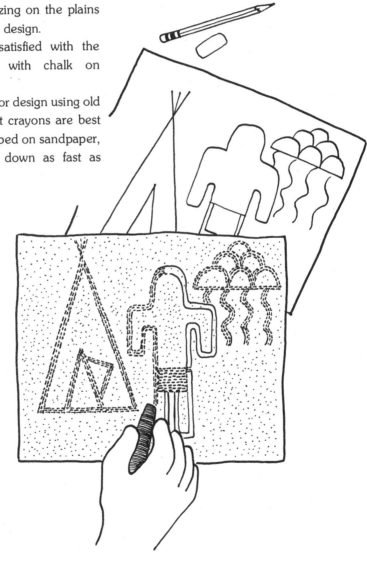

# XI. A Boy Named Rudolph

(In a chain story, something happens to one person or creature who makes something happen to someone else, who makes something happen to someone else, and so on. This chain story goes in a circle.

The leader reads the story twice. The children just listen the first time. During the second reading, children and leader name the next character together.)

One day a boy named Rudolph started to school.
He came to a puddle and stamped in it.
He frightened a frog
That jumped on the back of a woman
Who screamed, "A bear!" and called the police
Who sent out an alarm that worried the mayor
Who called the superintendent of schools
Who sent home all the children,
Including a boy named (Rudolph)
Who came to a puddle, stamped in it, and frightened a (frog)
That jumped on the back of a (woman)
Who screamed, "A bear!" and called the (police)
Who sent out an alarm that worried the (mayor)
Who called the (superintendent of schools)
Who couldn't do anything because he had already dismissed
   all the children,
Including (a boy named Rudolph!).

Nature is like a chain story, as a farmer found out in the following story.

# Owl, Old Friend

It was dusk. The sun was setting, but the sky was light. The old farmer sat beneath a spreading tree, drinking his tea. It was not ordinary tea, but tea rich with cream, just the way he liked it.

"Mmmm," he mused as he looked over his farm and saw his cows grazing in the meadows bright with clover. "How clever I am! I manage this farm all by myself. I am self-sufficient. Who could help me?"

"Who-oo-oo?" said a voice close by.

The old farmer looked up in the tree. There on a limb sat an old owl.

"Hello, friend," said the owl.

"Friend?" said the old farmer curtly. He didn't like being disturbed while drinking tea rich with cream. "Friend? How dare you call me friend, you homely creature?"

The owl opened his eyes and cocked his head to one side. He perked up his ears.

"Oh, go ahead," said the farmer. "Perk up your ears. Twist your beak. Make funny faces at me; but don't call me 'friend.'"

109

"But I am your friend," said the owl.

"How come?" asked the old farmer. "You hide yourself at dawn. You sleep all day while I work."

"I patrol your fields at night and catch or chase away the mice."

"Mice?" laughed the old farmer. "Who's afraid of mice? What harm can they do?"

"You'll find out," warned the owl. "I won't patrol your fields tonight. I won't catch your mice. Go catch your own mice!"

"Me? Catch mice?" yelled the old farmer. "Better to catch you! Get out of my sight!"

"I shall," answered the owl. "But you'll be sorry."

Away he flew, across the yard and into a hole in an old oak tree where he stayed all night.

After the sun was down, the mice who lived on the farm came into the fields. They looked around cautiously.

"Where's the old owl now?" whispered one mouse.

"You mean that ugly owl with pointed ears and twisted beak?" asked another.

"Who else?" answered the first. "He'll be the death of us yet if we don't watch out. But I don't see him flapping about tonight."

The mice waited and watched and watched and waited. But no owl appeared. At last one mouse called, "No owl tonight! We're safe! Let's have a feast!" Hundreds of mice came from their hiding places and ran all over the farm.

"Whoo-oo-oo," called the owl from his hole in the tree. "Old farmer, you'd better watch out! Mice are running wild. I can hear mice running all over your farm."

"Let them run," called the old farmer. "Mice aren't wolves. Mice don't kill cows."

The mice heard the call of the owl. They stopped for a moment. The owl stayed in the tree.

"Hey!" called one mouse. "I found bees' nests! Bees' nests in the ground."

"Bees' nests!" echoed the other mice. What could be more fun than digging up bees' nests? They scurried around digging up nests. The bumblebees woke up and flew away.

"Whoo-oo-oo," called the owl again. "The mice are getting wilder. They are digging up bees' nests. Your bumblebees are flying away."

"Let them fly!" called the old farmer. "Who cares? Bumblebees don't give honey. They only sting me. Who needs bumblebees?"

"You," called the owl.

"I need bumblebees?" cried the old farmer, now getting very sleepy with all the night talk.

"Yes, you," said the owl. "Your fields are covered with clover. Bumblebees pollenate your clover.
Your cows eat clover and give you cream.
You use cream in your tea.
Without bees you'll have no cream."

"Bosh!" said the old man. "Let the wind pollenate the clover. Now let me sleep!"

Night after night the owl stayed in his tree.

The mice ran in the fields and dug up bumblebee nests.

The bumblebees flew away to another farm.

By itself, the wind could not pollenate the clover.

The clover did not grow.

The cows had less and less to eat, so they gave less milk.

The old farmer had no cream for his tea.

Without cream, the tea tasted bitter. The old farmer longed for tea with cream.

"Oh, owl," moaned the old farmer one night. "I was wrong. You are my friend. I need you. Without you I'll drink bitter tea all my life."

"How's that again?" asked the owl.

"Owl," pleaded the old man, "I need you to chase mice who disturb the bumblebees
who pollenate my clover
that feeds my cows
that give me rich cream for my tea. Oh, owl, please be my friend again!"

"Gladly," said the owl, "because you know what?"

"What," asked the old farmer.

"Because I need to be your friend. I'm starving without the mice that chased your bees that pollenated your clover that fed your cows that gave you cream for your tea."

The old farmer laughed. "You're right, friend. All creatures need to live together."

The owl forgave the old farmer. He flew out of his hole and chased the mice. When the mice were gone, the bees returned and pollenated the clover. The clover

113

grew and fed the cows. The cows gave milk rich with cream. The old farmer sat at dusk beneath the spreading tree and drank his tea, very special tea rich with cream, just the way he liked it. He looked up at a branch on the tree and said, "Hello, Owl, old friend."

"Whoo-oo," said the owl and blinked in a friendly way.

> —A Russian tale translated from
> the Japanese and retold

## Owl Seed Mosaic

**Materials:** collection of seeds including flat, pointed, and very small ones; glue; and for a background—cardboard, poster board, or oak tag (a very heavy kind of art paper).

You can picture an owl in a mosaic, using a variety of seeds to make eyes, beak, and feathers.

Collect various kinds of seeds and dry them. You might include corn, pumpkin, watermelon, bean, squash, sunflower, apple, and other seeds. Also, if you can, collect smaller seeds such as wheat or other grain or birdseed. If you are unable to get small seeds, use rice.

Lay a few seeds of each kind on a table. Look at them. Push them together. Determine which seeds lie flat and look a little like feathers when placed next to one another and which seeds stick out like a beak or eyes.

Draw an owl on cardboard, oak tag, or poster board. Choose one kind of seeds for eyes. Brush glue on an eye of the drawing. Press seeds into the glue. Complete the other eye.

Glue in place the seeds you have chosen for the beak.

Fill in the outline of the owl, putting glue and then seeds into a small section at a time. Do not overlap seeds.

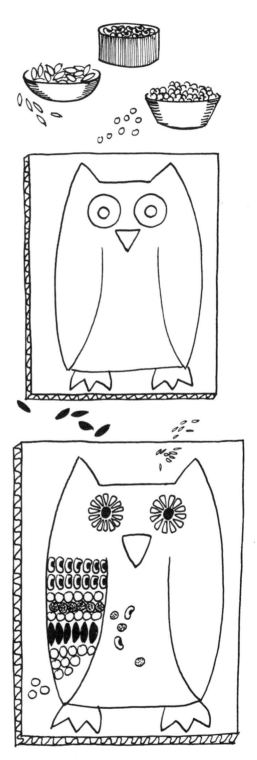

115

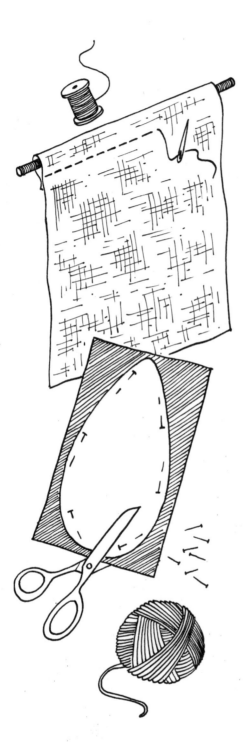

Add grain, small seeds, or rice anyplace where the cardboard shows through.

### Felt-Mouse Wall Hanging

**Materials:** fabric suitable for background of a wall hanging, a rod or heavy cardboard, decorative cord; for eyes, ears, and nose—gray felt, fabric or paper; for whiskers—yarn, pipe-stem cleaners or straw, glue, paper, pencil, felt-tip pen, staples or thread.

Choose a piece of felt, burlap, or other sturdy fabric for the background.

Stitch, staple, or glue one end of the fabric over a rod or a heavy cardboard strip. The rod should be slightly longer than the fabric is wide. Make sure that the fabric hangs evenly from the rod.

Make a paper pattern of the body of a mouse. It looks like a teardrop on its side. Using the pattern as a guide, cut out the shape of the mouse from gray felt or your chosen material. Glue it in the center of the fabric wall hanging.

Now complete the mouse. Glue a piece of yarn to one end of the shape to make a tail. Cut from paper or fabric a little circle for an eye, a triangle for a nose, and two small circles for ears.

Glue the pieces in place. One ear should be placed a little behind the other one.

Draw a mouth with a felt-tip pen.

Make whiskers out of yarn, pipe-

116

stem cleaners, or straw. Glue in place.

Cut a piece of decorative cord about three or four inches longer than the rod at the top of the picture. Fasten the ends of the cord to the ends of the rod. Now your wall hanging is ready to hang.

# XII. What Touched Me?

The leader copies in advance on three separate sheets of paper, acts to be pantomimed. When the group is together, the leader explains that volunteers will pantomime scenes. In each situation, a player is doing something intently. Something touches him. He is surprised, annoyed, or startled, as the case may be. Then he does something.

When the pantomime is finished, other players guess what caused the disturbance.

Each volunteer in turn receives a paper, reads it, pantomimes the act, and, when finished, asks, "What touched me?"

Three situations might be:

1. You are sewing or reading a book, very intent on what you are doing. Your dog nuzzles close to you. You look up. How do you feel when you see him? What do you do?

2. You are sewing or reading or writing a letter. A mosquito starts buzzing around your head. It keeps on buzzing and buzzing. How do you feel? What do you do?

3. You are seated barefooted on the grass or in the sand at the shore. You are reading a book and enjoying it. A small snake runs across one foot. How do you feel? What do you do?

When the pantomime acts have been completed, the leader may say, "Something is bothering John in the following story. Try to imagine how he feels."

# *John and the Twin Giants*

John was a tailor's boy. Sometimes he sat on a stool, sewing and sewing. At other times he sat cross-legged on the floor, sewing and sewing. But no matter how he sat, on a stool or cross-legged on the floor, flies buzzed around him on a hot summer's day.

Flies circled around his head, settled on his forehead, perched on his nose, flew into his ears. If he yawned or yelled, flies flew into his mouth. If he stopped sewing long enough to brush away the flies, his master called, "Stop yapping. Start sewing. You must finish that coat today. Lazy yokel, I have half a mind to let you go!"

John sewed on and on, and as he sewed, the flies became more than a nuisance. They became enemies. One day when he could stand the buzzing no longer, John stood up, grabbed a feather duster, and slashed through the air with a mighty blow. At his feet lay seven dead flies.

"I killed seven at one blow!" cried John triumphantly.

"Seven at one blow!" exclaimed his master who had just entered the room.

"Yes, seven at one blow!" John repeated.

"Seven at one blow is quite a feat. The world should hear about that," said his master jokingly.

"How can I tell the world?" asked John.

"I'll embroider a sash for you. It will say John Killed Seven at One Blow. Go into the world. Search for luck and fame."

"I'll do that!" said John, who at this point had almost forgotten that the seven he had killed at one blow were seven flies.

What began as a joke on the master's part became reality. The master embroidered an elegant sash for John who draped one end over his chest and the other end across his back and tied the two ends with a bow at his side.

"How bold I look!" said John, glancing down at the words John Killed Seven at One Blow.

"Think bold and use your wits," advised his master. He handed John some soft brown cheese as a departing gift. John put the cheese in his pocket, thanked his master, said good-bye, and started down the road toward adventure.

Everywhere he went people noticed his beautiful sash and read the words, "John Killed Seven at One Blow." No one asked, "Seven what?"

John, using his wits, kept the information to himself

and accepted with thanks the praise and hospitality that people offered. He had no need to eat his cheese so kept it in his pocket.

At last John came to a strange town. People stood in the square talking and yelling. Some people called out angrily. Other people cried. John could understand only two words above the babble—"twin giants." Evidently the people of the village had been terrorized by twin giants.

Suddenly someone spotted John and read the sign on his sash, John Killed Seven at One Blow.

"He's come! He's come!" cried someone. "A young man has come to save us from the giants."

"He's come!" cried someone else. "The giant killer has come. Long live John the Giant Killer!"

"Giant killer?" mumbled John. "I never killed a giant. The seven—," he added, pointing to the words on his chest. No one wanted to hear him say "seven flies," so he kept quiet.

"Seven!" the people shouted. "John killed seven at one blow. Surely he can kill two." No one asked John anything or told him anything.

"Go kill the giants!" a large man commanded as he pointed toward some woods. John could do only one thing: go into the woods.

"What'll I do if I meet a giant?" John asked himself

121

again and again. Then he repeated the words of his master, "Think bold. Use your wits. Think—" John stopped. What was that noise? A crick, crick, crick— John turned to the left. A little way off the path stood a giant, pulling up by its roots an oak tree as high as a castle.

"Wow!" said the giant when the tree was on the ground.

"Well done!" shouted John.

"Who's that?" yelled the giant.

"I, John, the strong man who killed seven at one blow," answered the tailor's boy, pointing to his embroidered sash.

"Strong man?" said the giant looking at John. "Who would guess it? Say, can you do this?"

The giant picked up a rock, lifted it above his head, and squeezed it. Water dripped into his mouth.

"Of course," said John. He reached into his pocket, pulled out his soft brown cheese, lifted it above his head, and squeezed it. Whey dripped into his mouth.

"You are strong!" said the giant grudgingly. "I need a strong man right now. Help me carry this little tree up that hill to my castle." The giant pointed first to the huge oak tree and then to a mountain in the distance.

"Gladly," answered John, thinking boldly and using his wits. "You take the trunk and walk ahead. I'll stay with the branches. The rear end of a load is usually heavier.''

"Agreed," said the giant. He swung the trunk of the tree up on one of his shoulders. "Get behind, little one. Tell me when you're ready. I can't see behind all the branches.''

John ran quickly to the rear and climbed up on top of the branches. "Ready!" he called.

"Let's go!" called the giant.

The giant tugged and pulled and tugged some more. John sat on top of the branches and whistled. The giant panted, stopped now and then, and gasped for breath.

John sat on the tree top, hidden by the branches, and whistled.

The giant grew more and more angry and somewhat worried as he walked. He kept thinking, "Here I am, a big man, tugging on this tree, panting, getting short of breath. There he is back there, a little man, carrying a heavy load, and he has breath to whistle."

The giant couldn't understand the situation. John explained nothing. He had promised to stay with the branches. He had said that the back end of a load is usually heavier than the front. Why not whistle as he rode on the tree?

The giant plodded on through the woods and up the mountain, carrying the tree and the little tailor. At last he reached the castle gate where he dropped the tree.

John jumped down from the branches, ran around the tree, and stood next to the exhausted giant who took one look at the little tailor, fresh and relaxed, and bellowed, "Brother!"

Out from the castle ran the twin who looked exactly like the first giant.

"Brother," gasped the tired giant, "I want you to meet the strongest little man on earth. He squeezed liquid from a rock. He carried the back end of this tree without getting tired."

"And I see," said the second giant, as he glanced at

John's sash, "he killed seven at one blow. I think he is the person we need to help us capture the king."

"Oh, no! Not that!" thought John. But what could he say now? What could he do? Nothing except bide his time, keep alert, and be determined to use his wits.

Day after day followed night after night as John lived under the watchful eyes of the giants. When the giants went to bed, John slept with the dog who barked each time any creature moved. When the giants ate, John sat on the table nibbling crumbs and scraps that the giants pushed off their huge plates. When the giants went for a walk, John rode on the shoulders of one or the other. Their giant steps were too long for the little tailor to walk with them.

One day the giants tied the dog to the door of their castle, picked up John, and started out on a long, long walk. They tramped through fields destroying grain, slushed through rivers upsetting boats, and crashed through forests knocking down trees that got in their way. The going was rough, even for giants, and the brothers grew weary. When they came to a small steep mountain jutting up from a plain, they stopped. John stood up on the shoulder of the giant who was carrying him. There, not far away, stood the castle of the king.

"Tired?" asked one giant of the other.

"Not really," came the answer, "but I think we ought to rest before we attack the castle."

"Agreed," said his brother. "The little one needs energy to kill seven at one blow once again." With these words, he set John on the ground. "Sleep tight, little one," he advised.

"Same to you," answered John.

The giants sat down side by side with their backs against the mountain, closed their eyes, and fell asleep.

John sat, trying with all his might to use his wits. Suddenly he spotted two flintlike stones on the ground beside him. "What can I do with these sharp stones?" he asked himself. An idea flashed into his head.

He picked up the stones, walked away from the giants, took careful aim, and threw one stone with all his might. The stone hit one giant in his temple.

Then, before the first giant was fully awake, John again took careful aim, threw the second stone, and hit the second giant in his temple.

The giants woke up, jumped to their feet, doubled their fists, and began to yell.

"You lout! You hit me!"

"No! You hit me! You tried to kill me!"

"You tried to kill me! You want to rule when the king is dead!"

126

"You want the money when the king is dead. I'll show you who gets the money."

With blows that made the earth shake, the brothers hit each other again and again in the head, in the stomach, below the belt. They wrestled with no holds barred. At first one was on top of the other. Then the other was on top of the first. On and on they fought.

John didn't stay to watch. He ran as fast as he could to the castle. The king, aroused by the great noise, was already at the gates with his archers.

"Giants!" yelled John. "Come!"

The king asked no questions but with his archers followed John back through the woods to the edge of

127

the plain. The archers drew their bows, ready to attack. But there was no need. Before them lay the two giants, bloody, bruised, bones broken—dead!

A large crowd of people who had followed the king and the archers broke into wild cheers. "John killed seven plus two!" they yelled.

"Not really," mumbled John. But no one heard him.

The king wanted an heir, so he made John his son.

The people wanted a hero, so they started legends about John.

All were happy. No one ever asked, "John killed seven what?" or "How did John attack the giants?" John never offered information that people didn't want to hear.

—Portuguese version of an old tale retold

## Giant Paper-Bag Stick Puppet

**Materials:** large paper bag, newspaper, sturdy stick or piece of lath longer than bag, string, construction paper, paste, tempera paint, staples; for hair if desired—strands of old rope or other material.

You can picture a giant by making a paper-bag puppet with a stick handle, a puppet that is easy to use when acting out a fight.

Stuff a large paper bag loosely with newspaper. Allow room at the bottom to tie the bag.

Put a sturdy stick or a piece of lath, longer than the bag, well into the stuffing, rearranging the stuffing if necessary.

Tie the bottom of the bag around the stick.

Paint ugly features on the bag or cut them out of construction paper, and paste them in place.

Cut out big paper ears if you wish. Staple them in place on the puppet's head.

Leave the puppet bald or give it hair by stapling on strands of old rope, strips of newspaper, or other material.

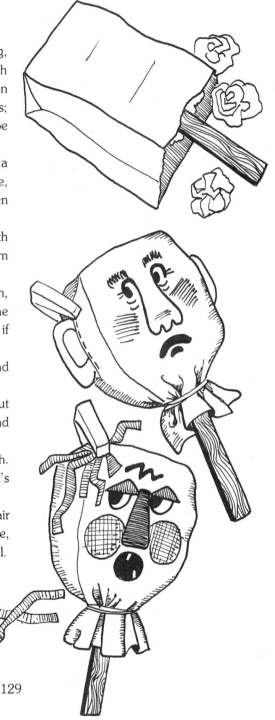

129

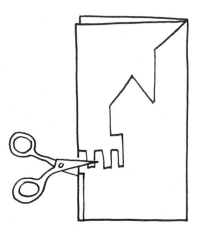

## Folded-Paper Picture

**Materials:** different colors or kinds of paper, paste, pencil; if desired—crayons and other materials for collage.

You can picture a castle or the twin giants with a folded paper cutout.

Fold a piece of paper in half. Draw a picture of half a castle with a dome, turrets, any type of construction you wish, on one side leaving the paper folded.

Cut out the picture of half a castle, do *not* cut on the fold. Open the paper. You will have a castle with identical sides.

Mount the castle on another piece of paper. Complete the picture by adding flags to the turrets, trees to the yard, figures to the foreground, or any other details to make an interesting scene.

The same method can be used to picture the identical twin giants. Fold the sheet of paper. Draw one giant so that part of his body is on the fold. He could be sleeping with his back or feet against the fold, or fighting with his fist against the fold, or walking with one hand on the fold.

Cut out the picture, being careful not to cut on the fold. When you open the paper, twin giants will appear.

Mount the double figure and complete the collage with more cutout figures or color the rest of the scene.

# Appendix I

## Other Uses of *Picture That!*

*Picture That!* will encourage leaders to look at children's books in a new way. A good book is more than a story to be read; it is a situation to be felt. It can open the way for dramatic and artistic creativity which helps children develop sensitivity to the natural world and to people around them, prods their intellectual curiosity, and spurs their imagination.

## Use with Other Stories

With a little thought, a leader familiar with *Picture That!* can use its methods and projects with other stories.

The index with its cross references helps in finding suitable activities, for example, among the dramatic activities:

"It's Christmas!" can be used with any story that expresses the joy of that season.

"A Great Big Something" is suitable with any ghost story.

"Guess What I Want to Be" can be used with a wishing story like "Hofus, the Japanese Stone-Cutter," who wanted in turn to be a rich man, a prince, the sun, a cloud, a rock, a stone-cutter. Or that activity can be changed to "Guess Who Is Coming to Dinner" in which children pantomime different kinds of people or animals—a dancer, a rabbit, a cowboy—to precede the reading of "Sometimes It's Turkey, Sometimes It's Feathers" by Lorna Balian, a story about an unusual Thanksgiving dinner guest.

Art activities can also be used with other stories. For example, a string-drawing net like the one Wild Rabbit used could picture the net that caught the lion found by Androcles.

A paper Christmas tree could picture "The Fir Tree" by Hans Christian Andersen.

# PICTURE THAT!

Paper-bag stick puppets of different sizes could picture the giant and Jack who climbed the beanstalk.

Fingerprint animals could picture the "Three Little Pigs" and the Wolf.

As an example of a story-activity plan, the story of the baby Moses found in the bullrushes might begin with the leader and children playing a pantomime game, "Guess What Our Family Does with Our Baby." Children can pantomime playing patty-cake, feeding baby with a spoon, rocking her, and so on.

After a few pantomimes the leader says, "The mother in the story about baby Moses had to do something unusual. As you listen, try to imagine how the family felt."

For an art activity after the story, the leader might choose one of the following:

a crayon-resist-paint picture of the bank of the Nile;

a collage of a basket among the rushes;

a string-paint picture of bullrushes along the Nile. Or she may choose another art activity.

Other ideas for art and dramatic activities can be found in the books listed in the second appendix.

## Working as a Group

The leader may wish to keep a group together for an entire period with a dramatic activity, story, and a group art project, such as creating a mural.

Pantomime songs (songs with motions, they were once called) and finger games are part of the American heritage. A leader can often recall or find one related to a chosen story. Sometimes a traditional pantomime game may be adjusted to fit a chosen story.

In choosing what kind of mural to create, consider the collage. Whether children are working in a group or on individual projects, the collage method is particularly satisfactory for beginners and for those unsure about their ability to draw and cut out.

Figures are drawn on separate sheets of paper, not on the paper that will be the final picture. If a child doesn't like the result, he discards his drawing and tries again without affecting the big picture. Children of different ages and with

132

different degrees of talent can work together on a collage, each making different figures.

A case history may show how a group of children, ranging from four to eight years old, worked to picture a story about monkeys and crocodiles that lived near an island where mangoes grew.

Before the story was told, the group looked at a picture of a crocodile and learned that it can grow to be twenty feet long. The leader and several children measured out twenty feet on the floor and extended a string the length. It was evident that the crocodile couldn't get into the room the group was using without bending his body around a corner or moving diagonally across the room.

Two children held the ends of the string, one to represent the head and the other the tail of the crocodile. A third child stradled the string.

The leader said, "Imagine how you'd feel if you were a little monkey, smaller than Brian (the child's name), riding on a crocodile as long as our string."

Then the group sang the old humorous action song "The Lady and the Crocodile" which is about a smiling woman who rides a crocodile she claims is tame, only to end up inside, behind its smile. Actions include hand motions, waving, winking, and smiling.

After the story the leader rolled onto the table white shelfing paper as long as the mural was to be. Everyone talked about what should go into the picture and what each should do.

One child colored the river and grass.

A talented girl nimbly drew and cut out monkeys while other children drew and cut out crocodiles.

Two others made trees and pasted them on each side of the river.

No attempt was made to produce figures in correct proportion.

The leader and the four-year-old snipped pieces of orange paper and pasted mangoes to the tree. Suddenly the four-year-old began to paste odd pieces of paper around the base of the tree.

"They're flowers," she explained. Indeed they did look like masses of jungle flowers. There were none pictured in the book.

# PICTURE THAT!

At the end of the period the children drew lots to determine who could take home the mural. The four-year-old won.

"Did you make that picture?" her grandmother asked in amazement.

"I made part of it," explained the child. "This and this." Then she began to tell the story.

## Children of Different Ages and
## Different Abilities Using Same Basic Art Activity

A group of children of different ages and with different abilities can work individually at the same basic art activity producing results satisfactory to each.

A case history may illustrate how an activity helped each child in such a group develop emotionally, socially, and intellectually.

A group of children were gathered with a leader and a teen-aged assistant while parents attended church services. The program was planned for children aged five through seven; but a four-year-old and an eight-year-old wanted very much to join and were allowed to do so.

The program centered around a picture-book story of what happened on a snowy day. After a little conversation about the snow outside, the group played a pantomime game: What Am I Doing Outdoors on This Cold and Snowy Day?

A child pantomimed an activity. Others guessed what he was doing. For example:  A child threw a snowball.

A child pulled a sled.

A child made "an angel in the snow" by lying down on his back and moving his arms up and down to make a pattern of wings.

A child walked in high drifts.

A child slipped and fell.

After a few pantomimes had been enacted and guessed, the leader read the story. She then told the group that she would like each one to make a collage of what might happen on a snowy day. They could illustrate the story, show themselves doing something on a snowy day, or make a picture of what they saw when they looked out the window.

## APPENDIX I. OTHER USES OF PICTURE THAT!

She gave each child a sheet of blue construction paper and half a sheet of white, asking them to paste the white on the bottom of the blue sheet to represent snow.

She asked a question, "Does snow always lie flat on the ground?

"No, it drifts."

"Cut the snow paper to look like drifts if you want to."

Jeff, an eight-year-old boy with remarkable talent, asked if he could make a picture about something he would like to do.

"Of course! Go ahead."

Jeff cut his white paper as suggested and pasted it in place. Younger children watched and then copied his action. From that point on, each child worked on his own project, not trying to follow what Jeff was doing.

Jeff started his collage with a small triangle. Intently he measured, cut, measured, snipped, and pasted. Sometimes he drew a part before he cut it out and pasted it in place.

At last there emerged a knight in full armor on a black horse, galloping across the snow. The initial triangle was the visor on the knight's helmet which evidently had caught Jeff's attention when his family visited a museum.

Jeff had produced a work of art, a picture any parent would like to display. He had developed socially and intellectually. He had—

related an art activity to an object he had seen;

creatively pictured it in a new setting;

shown tolerance as he listened to a story considered a little young for his age group;

accepted basic directions and followed them without arguing;

helped less-talented children by demonstrating how to get started.

At no time and in no way did Jeff pooh-pooh the efforts of others as he forged ahead on his own project, thus developing and practicing sensitivity and social maturity.

Meanwhile, Lucie, a four-year-old in the group, had been very, very busy. She laboriously covered all the white paper with paste, seeming to enjoy the gooey feel. Without help, she placed the white paper on the bottom of the blue sheet and then rubbed and pounded it, producing a kind of rhythm of

135

her own. Carefully she wiped up the extra paste oozing out of the edges with a paper towel.

She drew and then cut out a boxlike house and pasted it in place.

Then Lucie tried a few times and decided that she just couldn't cut out a roof that fit her house. The fact that she saw that her roofs were either too large or too small was an exercise in perception. At last she turned to the leader who cut out a roof for her.

Lucie laid the paper roof on her house, made sure that it fit, and pasted it in place. She drew a door and windows on her house.

Then she picked up a black crayon and drew lines back and forth on the white paper. "I walked in the snow," she explained. "It looks dirty."

Lucie did not produce a piece of art, but her art activity helped her grow in many ways. She had—

listened to a story;

related the story to her own life and interpreted it in her own way;

listened to directions and followed them;

developed independence as she started to work;

accepted help from an adult only when needed;

developed her sense of feel as she worked with gooey paste;

developed the small muscles of her hands as she cut, rubbed, pounded, and drew with a crayon;

developed perception;

developed socially as she talked to other children and observed what they were doing;

experienced success—a distinct aid to good mental health.

Lucie had produced a picture that delighted her completely and told her own story. She was as proud of her snowy scene as Jeff was of his knight on horseback—and with good reason!

# Appendix II

## Books That Can Help

Hundreds of excellent picture books and anthologies of children's stories are printed every year. Many old stories remain inspirational and fun, year after year. A list of picture books or a list of individual stories that can be used with art and dramatic activities would be too long to print in a book of this kind and would soon become obsolete. Part of the adventure of being involved in a story-activity program comes in perusing available books and chosing a perfect one for a program at hand.

Dramatic and art activity books are specialized, but the material and methods can be modified to meet many needs.

### Speech and Dramatics Books

Carlson, Bernice Wells. *Act It Out.* Nashville: Abingdon Press, 1956.

————. *Let's Pretend It Happened to You.* Nashville: Abingdon Press, 1965.

————. *Listen! And Help Tell the Story.* Nashville: Abingdon Press, 1973.

Grayson, Marion. *Let's Do Fingerplays.* Robert B. Luce, Inc., 1962.

Jacobs, Frances E. *Finger Plays and Action Rhymes.* New York: Lothrop, Lee & Shepard, 1941.

Tashjian, Virginia A. *Juba This and Juba That.* Boston: Little, Brown, 1969.

————. *With a Deep Sea Smile: Story Hour Sketches for Larger or Small Groups.* Boston: Little, Brown, 1974.

### Art Books

Alkema, Chester J. *Creative Paper Crafts in Color.* New York: Sterling Publishing Co., 1967.

————. *Masks* (Little Craft Book Series). New York: Sterling Publishing Co., 1971.

Borja, Corinne and Robert. *Making Collages.* Chicago: Albert Whitman & Co., 1972.

# PICTURE THAT!

Brock, Virginia. *Piñatas*. Nashville: Abingdon Press, 1966.

Carlson, Bernice Wells. *Make It and Use It*. Nashville: Abingdon Press, 1958.

————. *Make It Yourself*. Nashville & New York: Abingdon-Cokesbury Press, 1950.

Cutler, Katherine N. *From Petals to Pinecones* (A Nature Art and Craft Book). Lothrop, Lee & Shepard, 1969.

Enthoven, Jacqueline. *Stitchery for Children: A Manual for Teachers, Parents, and Children*. New York: Van Nostrand Reinhold Co., 1968.

Fiarotta, Phyllis. *Sticks & Stones & Ice Cream Cones*. New York: Workman Publishing Co., 1973.

Johnson, Pauline. *Creating with Paper*. Seattle: University of Washington Press, 1958.

Krinsky, Norman, and Berry, Bill. *Paper Construction for Children*. New York: Van Nostrand Reinhold Co., 1966.

Pflug, Betsy. *Pint-Size Fun*. Philadelphia: J. B. Lippincott Co., 1972.

Rainey, Sarita R. *Wall Hangings: Designing with Fabric and Thread*. Worcester, Mass.: Davis Publications, Inc., 1971.

Sattler, Helen R. *Recipes for Art and Craft Materials*. New York: Lothrop, Lee & Shepard, 1973.

Metcalf, Edna, ed. *The Trees of Christmas*. Nashville: Abingdon Press, 1969.

Wiseman, Ann. *Making Things: The Hand Book of Creative Discovery*. Boston: Little, Brown, 1973.

# Index

# PICTURE THAT!

# INDEX

# INDEX